Mark was thrown off his farm in Zimbabwe and wrote a detailed account of this in his book *SCRAMBLED AFRICA*. As a result he was forced to leave that country. The considerable success of this book has prompted him to write a book of short stories. He now lives in Dorset, England with wife, Nikki, and dog, Jessy.

Dedication

This book is dedicated to my family.

Many thanks to Sir Antony Milbank for writing a foreword.

Mark Milbank

ONLY HORSES AND FOOLS

AUSTIN MACAULEY
PUBLISHERS LTD.

A CIP catalogue record for this title is available from the British Library.

ISBN 978 178455 033 2

www.austinmacauley.com

First Published (2014)
Austin Macauley Publishers Ltd.
25 Canada Square
Canary Wharf
London
E14 5LB

Printed and bound in Great Britain

Contents

Foreword

by Sir Anthony Milbank

A collection of anecdotes and real life experiences drawn from Mark's long life in South America, Africa and back in England. Typical innocent, black humour from a man who while loving life and people is unable to hide his deep despair for the unfolding tragedy of Zimbabwe.

4

A Zimbo in Dorset

I arrived in Dorset in early January this year after living for 63 years in Africa. Ninety-five percent of Africa is a third world country. Dorset is in a first world country. There *is* a difference. Africa has sunshine and servants but not much works very well. Dorset in January is bloody cold, you do everything yourself and most things work pretty well – that is if you know which buttons to press. I did not.

I had to leave Zimbabwe after Mr Mugabe relieved me of my farm and I wrote a book telling the world how he had done it to me and many other very capable farmers. I was, perhaps , a little too truthful and as soon as the book, called *SCRAMBLED AFRICA*, was published I was advised to leave pretty quickly as Mr Mugabe and his cronies do not like the world to know what they have done to ruin a wonderful country.

Over the years I have visited England but always on holiday and usually in summer. As such one's host always did the washing up, let you use his telephone, lent you his car and generally saw that you were well looked after. Now I suddenly had to look after myself and in mid-winter as my wife remained in Zimbabwe to clear up the mess I had left. A kind [and very brave or stupid] friend of my sister said he would lend me his house for six weeks while he went on holiday in the sun in Australia. I had never met him before but he galloped through a few incomprehensible instructions about how to heat the house, which alarms to put on and when and where to put the rubbish on Tuesdays. He then handed me the key to his house, jumped into his car and disappeared to the airport.

Gingerly I entered the house. It was freezing cold. I looked at a small white box on the wall of the kitchen and noticed a lot of red lights flicking at me. I pressed one of them and a roaring sound filled the room. I quickly pressed it again and peace returned. It was still very cold so I decided to go out to my borrowed car and get some more clothes. As I opened the door there was a terrifying screaming coming from somewhere inside the house. I slammed the door shut but the screaming continued. The alarm! It must be the alarm. I tore round the house trying to remember what I had been told to do in these circumstances. Hidden deep in a cupboard was another white box. Frantically I pressed a selection of numbers which I thought I had been told would stop this racket – it didn't. Then the telephone started ringing, the dog next door started barking and a car screamed to a halt outside the front door. I rushed up to the driver in a panic and he calmly entered the house, pressed the right buttons to silence the alarm, answered the telephone and told the police to stay where they were, told the dog to shut up and introduced himself as my neighbour and friend of the house owner. He patted me on the shoulder, smiled and drove off.

I re-entered the house casting nervous glances in the direction of the two little white boxes. It was still cold so I approached the stove hoping to cook up something warm. I was confronted by a flat, shiny surface covered in a few circles and other hieroglyphics. It did not look remotely like a stove to me but the only word written on it near one of the circles said 'start' so I pressed it and six red spots suddenly blinked at me. I pressed one of these and some numbers appeared and the surface became hot. Great! I made myself some soup [out of a packet which is about the limit of my cooking]. This warmed me up a bit and I wanted to turn the stove off. I looked at the shiny surface and all the glowing red lights plus the one word 'start'. No hint of words like 'stop' or 'off'. I looked for some kind of switch – nothing. I stabbed my finger on a selection of the hieroglyphics but all remained obstinately red. I wandered round the kitchen for a bit trying to keep warm then glanced back at the stove and found that all the red lights now had a large 'H' beside them. I presumed that this stood for 'HELP' so tried to telephone my sister. The battery on my cell phone was flat and I did not have a connector to recharge it. She lived fairly near and had given me the keys to her house so I drove over. She wasn't there so I let myself out of her house and tried to lock the front door. The key would not turn. I turned it clockwise, then anticlockwise. I tried pressing the handle down and turning the key both ways. Nothing worked so I went back into the house and rang my niece on the house landline. 'Lift the handle up' she said. Oh!

I drove back to my borrowed house and peered cautiously into the kitchen. No little red lights blinked at me from the stove and later I learned that the 'H' stood for 'Hot'. I knew that! Stoves are meant to be hot aren't they? I wanted to know how to turn the ruddy thing off.

Next I was told I had to switch the fridge on. Personally I could see no reason to do this at all – anything just left on the kitchen table would be covered in permafrost in a very short time unless I could get some heat into the place. It took me 24 hours to find the switch for the fridge which was cunningly hidden behind a pile of cookery books. I then put some food in it to keep it slightly warmer than on the kitchen table.

I was not doing very well so decided to make some phone calls on the house landline. I had learned to use a computer in Zimbabwe – sort of – so tried to ring some advertised numbers so that I could get a computer up and running. I had been advised to use a 'dongle' as that would not require a telephone connection and, as I would be moving out of this house, this seemed to be a good idea. I phoned the advertised number to register with the dongle makers and arrange how to pay the sum of £15 per month which would allow me to use their cunning invention. I felt that £15 was a very moderate fee and the use of my newly acquired Visa card would arrange this pretty promptly. Three days later I was still trying to arrange the regular transfer of the vast sum of £15 from my account to the dongle makers. For starters it took at least ten minutes and the pressing of a vast selection of numbers on the telephone just to get a human, live voice. When I finally was ensured that the voice could actually reply to me I discovered that I could not understand a word it said.

I don't know if dongles are made in Pakistan but it appeared that all the guys who had to tell me how to pay for the thing spoke in a very strong, soft Pakistani accent. I have nothing against Pakistanis – they are very good cricketers and hard working, industrious citizens but I cannot understand them on a dodgy cell phone. As far as I could gather they would not let me pay them £15 until I had answered the sort of third-degree interrogation usually reserved for international spies. By the time this was finished my cell phone had run out of money and so, on ringing back, I had to go through the whole thing again.

At the end of the third day, by which time a selection of Pakistanis knew my entire life history, future prospects and the colour of my Great Aunt's eyes, I was finally asked for the numbers on my new Visa card. I think he said "Hold on while I check if it is valid. I held on [and my breath]. Was I finally going to be allowed to pay £15? The tension was unbearable. But no, I was informed [I think] that the card had not yet been registered – 'Good bye.'

The weather did not improve and the cold played havoc with my bladder. I had to make frequent dashes to any convenient loo, wrestle my way through the vast selection of clothes that I now had to adorn myself with and then search for a very small, very cold, unhappy 'dongle'!

Perhaps I should have risked Mugabe's prisons after all!!

2

A Zimbo in Patagonia

Having failed to get into Cambridge University after leaving school, my parents packed me off to Argentina to learn a bit about ranching as it seemed that I was incapable of learning about anything academic. I flew down to Cape Town and was soon deposited on a cargo boat bound for South America in general.

After ten days we reached Rio and I had my first look at South America. The entrance to Rio harbour is truly magnificent and modern visitors who jet in miss the build-up and anticipation of arriving in this exciting city.

Being a cargo ship, we spent three days in Rio and I went ashore all day and every day. I had very little money but this did not seem to be a problem; I walked everywhere and met a lot of very friendly people. These days if one is chatted up by casual acquaintances in a café or on the street one would be suspicious of some ulterior motive, but then it seemed quite natural and I really do not think that the people I met in these situations wanted anything except a chat to someone from another country. I had precious little to offer them except that.

I took the cable car up to the top of the Sugar Loaf, where it broke down, fortunately at the top and not dangling halfway up. However it was touch and go getting back to the ship before it sailed. I wonder if it would have waited for me. I wonder if the crew would even have noticed my absence, or just thought I was groaning on my bunk again! We moved slowly down the coast to Santos where we spent another three days. Santos is the port city for Sao Paulo and not in itself very exciting. Its main claim to fame is that the famous footballer, Pele, came from there. I would have liked to have a look at Sao Paulo but could not afford the bus fare. Another day or two and we were in Montevideo, the capital of Uruguay. We did not spend long there, much to my relief, as by now I was keen to arrive at my destination. Up the River Plate we sailed and finally docked in Buenos Aires, or BA as it is universally known.

There was a lone, lean figure walking up and down the quay as we arrived, and a shout and a wave revealed that he was Waldron's man come to meet me – a good start because Waldron's were the company I was supposed to be working for. It did not take long to get my one suitcase cleared through customs and Frankie Matthews was soon driving me through the streets of BA to the Waldron head office at 427, Bartholomew Mitre. He wanted to park the car more or less in front of the office entrance but the parking place was just too small for the length of the car, so he reversed in and pushed the car behind him back a bit, then forward, pushing that car on a bit, until he could just squeeze in. When I asked if this was normal procedure, he assured me that it was. All cars in BA had reinforced bumpers and it was an unwritten law that you did not put your handbrake on. It made for very efficient tight parking!

Eric Waldron greeted me. He ran the BA office, which was headquarters for the six or eight large estancias which the company owned, scattered throughout Argentina. He was a large avuncular man who immediately made me feel welcome. He summoned his secretary and told her to send a telegram to my parents saying that I had arrived safely and sat me down in an empty office and told me to write a letter home. All very thoughtful. At the end of the day I was taken to the very attractive Waldron house in the upmarket Hurlingham suburb.

I was to stay here for five days, during which time I was royally looked after. I attended a Catholic wedding, was taken to watch polo at the Hurlingham Club, went riding at the same smart club and went out to dinner with members of the Waldron staff on most evenings. Hurlingham was a very smart, English-style club with beautiful spacious playing fields, including at least six polo grounds. It all looked great until I rode round behind a line of trees surrounding these polo grounds, where I was horrified to see piles of dead horses – polo ponies to be more exact. They had just been dumped there and with no scavengers like jackals and vultures in Argentina, there they remained, providing food for a few crows and mangy dogs.

The Waldrons also had a very pleasant daughter called Pam and a resident friend called Ray Galley [Ray in this case was a girl], so things were looking pretty good. BA, in these circles at least, was very English. Spanish was the national language, of course, but so far I had not really had any reason to try out the little Spanish I had tried to learn on board ship. When going out to dinner one was not expected to start eating until about eleven-thirty, so this led to some pretty late nights, and consequently some lateish mornings. It was not until the sixth morning that I discovered where I was really going. I had begun to think that perhaps I was to be employed as resident gigolo for Pam and Ray. No such luck. "Would you like to spend a few months on our place in Patagonia?" Eric asked me over a nine-thirty breakfast. I could hardly say, "No, I would rather stay here entertaining your daughter," could I? And, anyway, I did actually want to get on with what I had come to do – see a bit of Argentina.

Estancia Condor was the Waldron 'place' in Patagonia. It was a huge sheep farm with the eastern boundary the Atlantic Ocean, the southern boundary the Straits of Magellan and the western boundary Chile. It was big, it was cold and, above all, it was windy. Nothing grew much higher than six feet and those bushes were all bent at an angle of 45 degrees, driven by a fierce wind coming straight from the South Pole. In the old days the estancia had its own port, and a ship came all the way from Darwin, in Lancashire, to pick up the Condor wool clip. There was enough wool to fill the ship! These days there was no less wool, but the clip was transported to nearby Rio Gallegos where it was taken on a much larger ship, together with wool from other estancias in the area. I was amused by the name of the estancia – "Condor," because the Swahili word for sheep is kondo.

Patagonia is a huge remote area, and only really suitable for sheep, so far as farming is concerned. There is a bit of wild life and a few dinosaur sites, and also some quite spectacular scenery. Few Argentineans actually live there – they rightly think it is too cold – and most of the labour was Chilean. [I suppose if you come from Chile you do not mind the climate being a bit chilly]. I arrived early in the morning at Rio Gallegos after a very bumpy flight on an ancient Dakota. The doors were opened and I stepped out into the coldest wind I had ever known. I still had moderately smart city clothes on and was pretty keen to get right back on to the old crate. Being an internal flight, there were no customs or immigration, so I picked up my suitcase and looked around. It was about six-thirty and no sign of life anywhere.

Suddenly my non-existent Spanish was in immediate demand. It did not help much, but I did manage to hitch a lift into town and was dumped at the only hotel. Not much was going on there either, but at least I got out of the wind. I found an empty dining room and sat around hoping someone might appear and give me a cup of coffee. A bleary eyed, bubsy woman finally appeared and babbled some incomprehensible Spanish at me. I thought that 'coffee' was a fairly universally understood word, particularly in a dining room at breakfast time, but it took an inordinately long time to get my message through and even longer before a brackish substance was put in front of me. I sat over this feeling cold and unwanted. It was abundantly clear that my Spanish was not going to be a great deal of help in solving my current predicament, which was: where is Estancia Condor, how do I get there and is anyone expecting me?

Bubsy woman reappeared [still in her night attire] and babbled some more Spanish at me. I smiled and shook my head. We were getting nowhere. Time passed, as time does, and somewhere around ten-thirty a large, brand new Chevrolet truck drew up in front of the hotel and a red faced English sort of looking guy walked in. "You Milbank?" he asked, in English. "Yes," I replied, cleverly using the same language. "Ah! I've been looking for you." Why didn't you start with meeting the 'plane, I thought. Jim Lord, for such it turned out to be, was Waldron's 'man in Gallegos' [when in the know, one omits the Rio bit, it only means, 'river' anyway] and was actually a very nice man and took me to his office, gave me some real coffee and asked where my proper clothes were. By 'proper' he meant something that would keep the wind out. My mother had gone out of her way to buy me a good selection of new clothes prior to my embarking on this adventure, and most would have been admirably suitable for a summer in the south of France but Patagonia had not been part of the equation. I was woefully ill-equipped even to walk down the streets of the town without freezing to death.

The headquarters of Condor were some fifty miles away, and while debating how to get me there another brand new large Chevrolet truck screeched to a halt outside the office. Condor did not have many neighbours – there is not much room between the Atlantic Ocean, the Straits of Magellan and Chile for any – but there was one, and it was this one who now strode into Jim's office. Alan Fenton was in town for some shopping and agreed to drop me off at Condor. The journey was fascinating in its way – miles and miles of NOTHING – huge, wide, windswept expanses of, well, nothing. Grass, of a kind, I suppose, but nothing else. I didn't even see any sheep and this was what the whole place was supposed to be about. I could quite understand why sheep would need a really good fleece to keep warm in this climate, but where were they? I asked Alan and added that they must be profitable if the brand new American cars were anything to go by. It seemed that one sheep needed all of five acres to survive here, so one did not see many when driving along the main road. As to the cars, it seems that the Argentine government realises that Patagonia is such an unpleasant place to live that any-one who does choose to can buy goods duty free.

Shortly before dark, the endless plain of nothingness suddenly dipped into a sheltered valley and there, nestling at the bottom, was a large house followed by a line of smaller ones, culminating in a huge complex of sheds. We headed for the large house, home of the Condor manager, Eric Davis and his wife, Joan. I should, perhaps emphasise at this point, that Condor and the whole Waldron empire was very much English-owned. Peron had been ousted from power a few years earlier but during the time of his rule foreign-owned businesses had come under a lot of pressure and many had closed down. Waldron's had survived and, while they employed local labour, or peons, as the farm workers were called, most of the top managers were still basically British.

Eric Davis certainly was, although he had lived in Argentina most of his life. He welcomed me and gave me a drink consisting of gin and Cinzano in equal quantities in a small glass. He then said that I could spend a couple of nights with his number two, before moving down to the main mess.

Number two was a lively little Scotsman called David Mackenzie. He had a somewhat browbeaten wife, but no children. They lived in the next house down from the main house, the 'Casa Grande,' as it was referred to, and it was there that I spent the weekend. Mackenzie took me to meet the other members of the mess where I was going to be permanently based. There were some ten or twelve of them, not peons but under-managers, accountants, mechanics etc. and a couple of young British Argentinians who were cadets in the same way that I was. The place, known as the 'comedor chico,' [small dining room] was run by a very cheery couple, called Augustine and Doña Ramon, who cooked for us and generally kept the place clean. One problem became immediately apparent – they all spoke Spanish and mine had so far proved woefully inadequate. To be fair, a couple of them did speak a bit of English, but I was going to have to learn fast or feel very left out.

On the Monday morning I reported for work and moved down to the 'comedor chico'. Before that, Mackenzie had very kindly lent me some warmer clothes, the most important of which was a thick leather jacket which he said would keep the wind out. There was an English-speaking foreman or 'capataz' called Speke. He had been on Condor most of his life and was a fairly grumpy character. I suppose most people would be, if they had spent most of their lives in a howling gale. Speke eyed me with some apprehension, not because he was frightened of me – far from it – but because, I suspect, he was wondering what the hell he was to do with me. "Can you ride?" he asked dubiously. Well, I could, I played polo didn't I? But Argentina boasts some of the finest horsemen in the world, and riding is very much the macho thing to do, particularly on the large estancias, so I was fairly cautious in my reply. "A bit," I said. "Well, go with Antonio, catch yourself a horse and spend the day with him, he will be checking on the rams in the Home paddock."

Antonio was a Chilean shepherd. He could speak no English and clearly did not want to be lumbered with a ruddy 'gringo' all day ['gringo', is the derogatory term used for foreigners, particularly English men]. He took me first to a sort of tack room, where there were countless halters and bits and sort of bridles made out of rawhide but no saddles that I could see. Surely we did not have to ride bareback, the locals could not be THAT macho. Antonio gave me a halter and bridle, and then indicated a wooden frame and a heap of sheepskins all tied up with a variety of thongs. This, it turned out was the saddle.

I staggered off with this lot to a huge corral where there were some fifty or sixty horses milling around. Several other men all in long baggy trousers, leather aprons and the required thick leather jackets, were also milling around trying to catch some of these horses. Antonio pointed to a sturdy looking dark brown gelding with patches of white on it. He stood maybe fifteen hands. How did one catch a Patagonian horse that was rushing around with sixty others? Lasso? I did not have one and did not know how to use it anyway. Hand full of sugar? I did not have that either. I stole a glance at the others but they were all watching me! I slowly approached the horse, which gave me a fairly patronising look before disappearing into the jumble of his mates. It suddenly dawned on me that there were several fifteen-hand brown geldings with patches of white on them, so which was the one I was meant to catch? It did not actually matter very much because I could not catch any of them and was not receiving any help from the assembled watchers, who were now rolling cigarettes and smirking among themselves. Antonio was nowhere to be seen.

Quite how long this pantomime would have continued, I do not know, because it ended suddenly as Speke hove into view. All was then activity. Cigarettes were dropped, halters produced and horses caught. Antonio appeared with a sweet smile on his face leading a stocky brown and white gelding of about fifteen hands. He even helped me put on the unwieldy saddle and showed me how to do it up, not with one girth but two, and then a surcingle over the top to hold the sheepskins in place. Gingerly, I mounted and found the unfamiliar saddle arrangement surprisingly comfortable. It was just as well it was, because I spent the next six hours sitting on it. It seems that there is a recognised way of catching these horses. You approach them with the halter open and held out in front of you. The horses are trained [some of them!] to stand still and allow you to slip the halter over their nose.

The Home paddock would not have been called a paddock in England. County, perhaps? It was one of the smaller ones on the estancia, but must have been all of five thousand acres and it took Antonio and me all day to ride round it and to check on as many of the thousand or so rams as we could. It had been comparatively warm trying to catch the ruddy horse because we were still in the sheltered valley where the headquarters was situated. Now we were out of the valley and benefiting from the full force of the wind, which is such a feature of Patagonia. I do not like wind and learned to loathe it over the next six months.

I went out with Antonio for most of that first week. Conversation never flowed very easily and even if we had both spoken the same language, this would have been difficult due to the noise made by the wind and the fact that we wrapped scarves round our faces.

I have been rude about the countryside but it was in fact fascinating and beautiful, in its own way. Nothing did grow above six feet, and that only in sheltered spots, for the rest it was rolling dry grassland which only got fifteen inches of rain a year. Every now and again one came across a lovely lagoon of fresh water, which was often full of duck, geese, snipe and other water birds. I had always been keen on bird shooting and managed to borrow a twelve bore and had several amusing Sunday afternoons around these lagoons while my companions were sleeping off their Sunday lunch.

When I had learned my way round a bit I was sent off on my own to check on the sheep. This was an all day business, Having [eventually!] caught one's horse from the pool that was driven in every morning, the rest of the day was spent inspecting fences, looking out for 'cast' sheep [that is sheep with a heavy fleece of wool that roll onto their back and cannot get up], checking that the windmills were working and attending to any injured sheep. This last being mostly 'fly blow,' which is any small cut being infected by maggots. It was not wildly exciting work once the novelty had worn off, but there was a bit of game around, notably guanaco, a kind of wild llama with a wonderful warm fleece and a type of ostrich called a rhea or avestruz [Spanish]. These often had large nests of eggs and it was a big bonus to find one of them as they were delicious to eat and chicken's eggs were not that plentiful.

There were two highlights during my stay. The first was lamb marking and the second was shearing. Lamb marking took place in the spring, a few weeks after the half million or so lambs were born. All this happened over a vast area and each flock of ewes and lambs had to be rounded up into a pen built in the corner of each paddock and the lambs caught, de-tailed, ear-marked and, if male, castrated. To do one paddock took some thirty men, divided into teams of ten, all day. One usually ended up some twenty miles from headquarters and there was obviously no time to go back as the whole exercise was conducted on horseback. It was a huge logistical exercise during which we camped out for six weeks.

The drill was that a team of horse-drawn wagons went ahead and set up camp. The riders, of whom I was one, got up at three-thirty in the morning, just as it was getting light, caught their horses [hopefully] which had been hobbled nearby and set off in three teams to round up a ten thousand acre paddock. Each team headed for a corner of the paddock, or camp, as they were called, where there was a permanent set of pens; pens that were probably only used once a year, for this very purpose. The rounding up was usually complete by about ten o'clock with all the ewes and lambs in that section of the camp now in one huge pen. The lambs were then sorted into a smaller pen and seven of the team would catch them and hold them up on a plank for the three most senior members of the team to do their worst; worst, that is, as far as the lambs were concerned. The lambs were then released to rejoin their mothers, which had been released and were waiting outside the pen to succour their little darlings.

Having rounded up the flock we would have breakfast before commencing the marking. This would consist of hot, sweet, black coffee, very dry brittle bread, called galleta, and as many lamb chops as you could eat, grilled over an open fire. These were totally delicious and, whenever I think of the best food I have ever eaten these always spring to mind. Part of the reason, obviously, was that I was young and ravenously hungry, having been working hard for several hours in cold weather, but my word, they were good!! I could easily eat twenty at one sitting.

Lunch would be eaten when we had finished the marking, usually around two o'clock, and would be exactly the same as breakfast, supplemented by lambs' testicles – equally delicious as long as you could close your mind to what you were actually eating. We then rode on to the new camp, which had been erected by the guys with the wagons who had picked up the tents from our old site and moved them to the new. On arrival we would unsaddle our horses, hobble them for the night, and give them a bit of hay [also brought by the wagons] but no hard food. We then had to make our beds, do our ablutions, have supper – same as breakfast and lunch – and collapse exhausted into bed at about seven-thirty.

There was a variety of tents. The peons had two large ones between them; the shepherds, who were one notch up the social scale, had one to themselves, then we cadets had our own, and there were just five of us. The boss, Eric Davis, had a tent all to himself, as befitted such a deity, and one of us had to be on call at all times in case he wanted anything. Our beds were pretty crude, being nothing more than a thin mattress on the ground accompanied by a selection of blankets and sheepskins. The boss, though, had a proper camp bed.

Despite the basic beds, it was VERY difficult to get out of them at three-thirty the following morning! It would still be dark, freezing cold and blowing a hurricane. First job would be to find your horse, which, although hobbled, could wander off quite a long way during the night. Then, with numb fingers you had to saddle it up and mount. I do not think that the horses liked being disturbed so early very much either, because they would often register their displeasure with a series of alarming bucks. This was bad enough because, being half-asleep anyway, all you wanted to do was hang on for dear life, but honour demanded that you beat your horse, which obviously made it buck more. This is another macho Argentinian custom, so, if my horse bucked, all eyes were on the 'gringo' to see that he did the required thing. We would change horses every three days, so the fourth morning was always a tense time. I never did fall off on these occasions, but there were some pretty close calls and the horses I got tended to get worse rather than better. I sometimes wondered who chose which horse I should be allocated.

There is an art to rounding up such large camps with ten riders. The first rider, called the pointero, goes off first and basically rides along the boundary fence pushing any sheep he sees further into the middle; the next rider follows behind and pushes them still further in, and so on until they all end up more or less in the middle of the camp and can then be driven to the pens. These sheep are probably only handled twice a year, so they are pretty wild. The pointero had the most ground to cover and I coveted this role as one had to go fast and so could keep a little warmer. The last guy to go did not ever get out of much more than a trot and spent a lot of time hanging around, getting colder and colder. Also, not knowing these camps, it was quite easy to get lost if one could not see the rider immediately ahead. As pointero, you at least had a fence to follow.

Lamb marking in Patagonia was certainly an experience and a challenge, possibly more fun looked back on than it was at the time. As my Spanish improved slightly, I got on very well with the other guys. Sure they teased me a bit but it was all in good fun and nothing malicious.

Soon after the end of lamb marking it was Christmas. Frank Waldron came down to stay in his house at the other end of Condor from where we were. His niece, Pam, and Ray Galley also came down to stay and we cadets were invited down for lunch. This was a rare treat. I do not think any of us had set eyes on a girl for months and we were sick of the sight of sheep. I had a bit of a head start on the others as I had met Pam and Ray in BA. Lunch was the traditional asada [barbecue in England, braai in Africa or barby in Australia!]. I think though that the asada wins in these stakes. A whole lamb is spitted over glowing coals and basted with a delicious sauce as it cooks. I have seldom tasted anything as good. I regret to say that having tasted this, we stole a lamb on a couple of occasions and had our own asadas when we were off duty. We salved our consciences by reasoning that there were still four hundred and ninety nine thousand, nine hundred and ninety eight lambs left [Eric Davis and Speke are certainly dead by now so I can at last come clean].

After lunch with the Waldrons I was keen to press home my advantage, so suggested a game of cricket on the lawn. This was something that I had been quite good at and I reckoned that the others would be quite bad at, mainly because they had never played it. Also, I suspected that the most senior of my fellow cadets had had something to do with the selection of my horses, so I was keen to get a bit of my own back on him.

A tennis ball was found, and even an ancient bat. We used a chair as a wicket and play commenced. I decided to bat fairly early on to show the others how it should be done, the idea being that they would then come in and make fools of themselves and I would be a hero in the eyes of the girls. There must have been about a dozen of us playing. Evan Williams, who had played a bit of cricket, was bowling, I was batting and Pam was standing at square leg. Evan's first ball to me bounced in the middle of the pitch and came slowly towards me at waist height, the ideal ball to hook. Hooking was one of my strongest points and I latched on to this ball as I have few others. It flew like a rocket straight at Pam and hit her on the protruding part of her chest [or to be exact, smack on the left tit!]. She collapsed, I rushed to her aid, the other girls screamed and confusion reigned supreme. Pam was carried into the house, the cricket game was abandoned and we five cadets slunk home. Far from being the hero of the hour, both myself and the game of cricket as a whole were roundly condemned. We were all invited up to the Casa Grande for dinner on Christmas Day – the only time I ever went there after my initial greeting. Such an occasion demanded a clean shirt and tie, neither of which had been necessary so far during my stay at Condor. I was horrified to discover that I could not do up the top button of my shirt or even the cuffs. I must have put on twenty or thirty pounds since my arrival. Having grown up in hot Africa, where one sweats a lot, I now found myself not sweating at all and eating probably more than I was used to. I was fit enough, but FAT! The evening was fun and we ate turkey rather than lamb, drank some very acceptable Argentinian wine and, after dinner, played billiards. I don't think I disgraced myself this time.

The next excitement was shearing. If lamb marking had been a complicated logistical exercise, it was nothing compared to getting every sheep on the place into the shearing shed at estancia headquarters. The whole exercise took some three months and I was there for all of it. To begin with I went out on horseback to help the shepherds round up the flocks and start driving them towards headquarters. All this began well before the teams of shearers started their work – they had to be guaranteed a continual flow of sheep through the shed. The only acceptable excuse for there being no sheep to shear was rain – you cannot shear wet sheep, as the fleece will rot in the bale.

Condor had its own team of shearers and an outside team was also hired. In the shed there were forty points all supplied with electricity for mechanical shears, so there were about forty shearers working most of the time. A small pen opposite these points contained some twelve sheep and a young, strong guy had to catch these sheep and hand them over to the shearer, whose only job was to shear them and shove them through a sort of trap door behind him, where they waited, shivering, in another pen ready to be counted out. I say 'only' job, but shearing sheep is probably the most tiring job there is. The whole exercise is conducted while you are bent double and you have to battle with a fresh animal every few minutes. Your arms must be strong and your legs even stronger, to say nothing of your back. Then you must also be pretty skilful, as no one wants to see a freshly shorn sheep squirting blood in all directions. The shearers were paid strictly per sheep sheared and the count for each guy was pinned up every morning. The best did about two hundred and fifty, the worst under a hundred. On average some seven and a half thousand sheep were sheared each day. The shed held three thousand five hundred, so it had to be filled at least twice a day.

For some six weeks I was the strong, young guy who had to keep the shearers supplied with sheep. There were four who we had to keep supplied and it was hard work, it meant that we had to catch, turn over and drag for some three yards approximately seven hundred sheep a day. From being fit and fat, I very quickly became very fit and thin. It was pretty warm in the shed, no wind and lots of animal and human heat bouncing around. Every hour or so the shearers would take a break, go outside and have a cigarette. This obviously meant that we could take a break as well. But it was a great opportunity to learn how to shear. After all, we had been watching it done by experts day in and day out. So while our four shearers relaxed, we strong, young guys were at liberty to grab a sheep and give it a go ourselves. It meant we did not have a rest, but it is amazing what one can do aged twenty.

Poor sheep, though. I was not very good to start with, but my shearers were keen to encourage me, because any sheep that I sheared [and which lived] was credited to their account. I did improve and on one of the last days I actually managed fifteen. That evening I went down to the shearers' camp and shared a couple of canyas [a type of fiery local brandy] with the guy whose place I had taken while he rested. He was one of the best shearers anyway, and with my help of an extra fifteen, it had made him top shearer for the day, a very coveted position and one over which a certain amount of money changed hands. He was teased, though, that he had needed a 'gringo' to help him reach the top spot.

All the wool had to be graded and baled, ready for export, so graders were specially employed and came to Condor from BA for the whole of the shearing. They all stayed at the comedor chico, which made it quite crowded, but led to a lot of parties. We worked every day, Sundays included, so it was a bit of a bonus when it rained, as it meant the shed could not be filled and consequently no shearing and no work for us. Rain was an expensive nightmare for the management, but we were not the management. Most parties took the form of the celebrated asada, outside in the long summer evenings, usually in some semi-sheltered spot, as out of the wind as possible. A lot of wine was drunk, usually out of those leather wine skins, which you point at your mouth, squeeze, and hope the resulting spurt of wine goes into your mouth. It does, if you have had a lot of practice. I had not had any practice, and would end up with a lot of cheap red wine up my nose, in my ear or, worst of all, in my eyes. I suppose it helped to keep me fairly sober, because I never managed to get much in my mouth.

Sheep that had been sheared tended to feel a little chilly. Most had been relieved of some twelve pounds of prime wool. If the weather remained fine it was all right and they soon adjusted and got on with the job of growing a new fleece. But, if the weather suddenly turned cold or, even worse, it rained as well, the wretched newly shorn sheep were dead pushed. In fact, a lot were just plain dead. This very scenario happened towards the end of shearing, when a smallish flock of old ewes huddled in the corner of a particularly windy camp the day after they had been sheared and some four hundred died. With all the activity everywhere else they were not discovered for several days, by which time they were turning blue and smelt to high heaven. Guess who was sent out to pick them up? Evan

Williams and I were given the job. We parked the lorry near this stinking pile and each grabbed two legs and attempted to heave the carcass on to the back of the lorry. Sometimes we succeeded, but more often than not the rotting blue skin on the legs came away in our hands and the stinking carcass just slid under the wheels, from where we had to retrieve it and manhandle it onto the back. Our evening meal of the inevitable mutton did not go down too well that evening.

After the shearing, the young rams had to be selected, either to be sold or to be retained for breeding. This is where the boss, Eric Davis, played a very active role. It was he who determined the fate of each ram [the rams had already avoided their worst fate: after all they were still rams]. There were some five thousand to select from and each of these had to pass through a race, with the boss standing back and looking at their conformation. They did not actually stop, so the boss had to make a snap decision. If he liked what he saw and wanted to keep that particular ram for breeding, he would shout out, "That one!" Upon hearing this, an agile youth on the other side of the race had to put a long red chalk mark down the back of the selected ram. I was that agile youth. Snap decisions are relatively easy to make if you only have to make two or three, but when it comes to five thousand, the maker of them can become a trifle confused.

We would start at the fairly civilised hour of eight-thirty and all would go very well for the first hour or so. The boss was a good man and knew his sheep. Then the occasional, "Sorry, no, not that one," would creep in. This would become, "No, no, no, I didn't mean that one at all, you'll have to get it back." Then, "No, you fool, I never said that one." And finally, "JESUS, can't you understand plain English, NOT that one." By this stage I was a nervous wreck tearing up and down the race, hauling back rams that had been wrongly marked, and making wild guesses as to which ram should actually be marked. At about half past twelve, when I was on my knees and the air blue with the boss's curses, he suddenly just walked away, jumped into his truck and drove off. I was left there feeling rather stupid. Speke appeared from nowhere and revealed a rare human side to his nature. "Don't worry, laddie," he said. "It's always like this when selecting rams. Go and get your lunch, but be back by two." From two o'clock to five-thirty it was the same pattern, quite organised to start with, but reaching a screaming crescendo by the end.

With the end of shearing, work on the estancia started to calm down, and, with winter approaching, sheep were returned to their vast camps to fend for themselves. With this scaling down of activities it was deemed that my invaluable services were no longer strictly essential and that the management of Condor could possibly spare me to help out on another estancia whose need was more pressing. Eric Davis, with tears in his eyes and choking with barely concealed emotion, told me that I was to leave and be re-deployed to another estancia.

3

A Zimbo in Argentina

So I left Condor and Patagonia and flew back to BA. It had certainly been an interesting stay and I suppose I had learned a bit. How much of it would be of any use to me back in Africa, I wondered. I had proved to myself at least, that I was perfectly capable of hard work, had learned a bit more Spanish and was able to get on with people from a very different background.

I was not met when I landed in BA but had been told to make my way to the Strangers Club. Here I stayed for about a week and explored BA on my own. It is an exciting city, which stays wide awake deep into the night.

Politics have never been Argentina's strong point and they were in the usual state of flux when I was there. Peron had been ousted some years before and the current incumbent of the President's office was the less than inspiring Frondizi. I attended the big annual agricultural show and listened to him open it. He, and various other important little men, made long rambling speeches while I stood in pouring rain. I was not impressed. Later that same night I got caught up in some street riots where protesters were demonstrating for the return of Peron. The 'man in the street' was still very pro-Peron or, more particularly, perhaps, the memory of Evita, his now dead wife, who had championed the masses while bankrupting the country. There were plenty of men in the street that night and the police and army chucked tear gas around and very unpleasant it was too. I slunk back to the Strangers Club with very red, sore eyes. Frondizi did not last long and Peron was eventually returned to power, but I do not think that my presence in the demonstration had anything to do with that.

It is, perhaps, interesting to note in passing, that even then, the Argies were pretty uptight about the Falkland Islands. Any large map depicting them had the official name scratched out and the Argentinian version, Islas Malvinas written instead.

One of the Waldron hierarchy called Roberts was kind enough to ask me to a big party he was holding for his daughter. I duly went and spent the night. It was quite fun, although I did not know a soul. Partly it was fun because most of the chatter was in English. I had not realised what a strain it had been speaking and listening only to a language that I partly understood. This, I think, made me talk rather too much and I suspect I was a crashing bore as I was dispatched back to the Strangers Club fairly rapidly next morning.

Soon after that, though, I boarded a train for Bahia Blanca, a city on the coast due south of BA. Here I was to travel inland to another of the Waldron estancias near a little village with the unlikely name of Lopez Lecube in the province of La Pampas. Eva Peron had been born in this province as the illegitimate, fifth child of a shopholder in a small village. After she married Juan Peron and later became Argentina's first lady, she tried to change the name of the province to Eva Peron, but failed to do so and La Pampas, or The Pampas, it remained. If you cannot find Lopez Lecube on the map, I am not surprised. It consisted of about three shops, a pub, post office and an enormous church built out of marble imported from Italy. The Waldron estancia pretty much surrounded this village and I was billeted with the manager, one Bob Skinner.

Bob Skinner was a Scotsman and, as such, spoke English [of a sort!]. He was, of course, also fluent in Spanish and was, in fact, married to a very pretty, very neurotic Argentinian girl called Elva. Elva was a city girl and did not take kindly to life on an estancia; she seldom ventured out of the house, indeed, seldom out of her bedroom until lunchtime. She had many urgent calls to return to BA and was really seldom there. Bob, who I called, "Mr. Skinner," was a good sort and, I think enjoyed having me around, as my background had a bit more in common with his than any of his immediate neighbours, or wife, who were all Argentinian. I lived in the main house with him but spent the day out with the gang. The main enterprises were cattle and sheep and my job was, in many ways similar to what I was doing at Condor, except that here we had cattle as well and I have always much preferred working with cattle than sheep. The cattle were lovely Herefords, not pedigree, but pretty high grade. The 10,000acre estancia was well fenced into paddocks each with its own windmill and subsequent water supply. Rain fell every month in acceptable amounts, the grazing was sweet and there was very little disease so it was little wonder that the cattle flourished as, indeed they do in a lot of Argentina.

To be honest, there was not a hell of a lot to do. I would catch and saddle a horse every morning and then be allocated two or three paddocks to check during the course of the day. My job was to see that the windmill was working OK, mend any broken fences and check on the stock, be they sheep or cattle.

I did attain one more skill. I use the word "attain," with some caution. I was tempted to say "master," one more skill, but this would have been a gross exaggeration! This skill was the use of a lasso. It was almost essential to know how to use one, because, if while checking the stock, you saw an animal with a problem you had to do something about it. It was nearly always too far and too time consuming to drive it to a corral, so you had to catch it right there and treat the problem. The most common problem in the summer months, which is when I was there, was "fly blow." This occurs when the animal suffers a small cut and flies lay their eggs in the wound. These eggs hatch into a type of maggot before becoming a fly and feed on the raw flesh. This is obviously very painful for the animal as the wound goes septic and it has to be treated as quickly as possible. The only way to do this was to catch the animal, tie it up and treat the wound with a special powder that we carried with us.

This was comparatively easy in the case of sheep – the tying up and treating bit I am referring to here – but quite another matter where cattle were concerned. With practice, one could handle a calf on one's own, but anything much bigger required two people. The art of roping and tying a small steer is one of the feature events at most rodeos throughout the USA and also in South America. It is a highly skilled operation but takes the experts something like ten seconds. It took me something like ten hours before I managed to catch and tie my first calf. This is why I use the word, "attain." I could do it, and during the rest of my stay in Argentina, improved considerably. It was a challenge and a lot of fun.

Perhaps I should give a layman's description of how this is done and just hope that no one who can really use a lasso ever reads this. A proper lasso is made out of one cowhide cut thinly into strips and made into an eight-strand rope. The hide has to come from a fat healthy cow and the plaiting of the lasso has to be done during moist, humid conditions. The 'puestero' who very generously made mine, said it also had to be done over the full moon, but I suspect this is stretching it a bit far. Onto one end is joined a stout metal ring and on the other a loop, thinner than the main lasso, with a leather button and eye. The total length varies, but is about forty feet long. The whole thing is elastic in that it can stretch by at least another foot. It is also incredibly strong.

The end of the loop is passed through the metal ring and then attached to the saddle on your horse. This can either be onto a horn on the pummel or to another ring at the top of the girth. You then mount the horse and pay out enough slack to make a noose some twenty feet round. The balance of the lasso is then held in three or four coils in your right hand with the actual noose dangling down to the ground. Now comes the difficult bit! You have to wave this lot round your head in the approved fashion as done by John Wayne [or his stand-in] in countless cowboy movies. This is not as easy as it looks – particularly if the horse objects to being clocked around the ears and tripped up as soon as it starts to move. Like all things, it is a technique and, after much practice, you can get it swinging round your head in a comparatively smooth arc.

OK, now you have to use it. The trick is to forget about the noose, but pretend that you just have a metal ring on the end of a rope and you aim this at your target. Having picked a target you let fly and if you have aimed well and true the metal ring homes in on this target and the noose of the lasso spreads out in front thus encircling it. You then jerk it taut and you have your quarry.

From the back of a horse you gallop after your calf and hope that it runs straight away from you. Then, standing up in your stirrups and uttering a blood-curdling yell, you hurl the metal ring at the back of the galloping calf and hope that the noose loops gracefully over its head. If it does, you immediately rein in your horse and the wretched calf is brought to a screaming halt with a noose wound tightly round its neck. If the calf does not run straight away from you it is much more difficult so, in my case, many flyblown calves remained flyblown!

Having caught the ruddy thing you then have to do something about it and here the co-operation of the horse is vital. An untrained horse would take a very dim view of being attached to an active calf, so the horse you use has to have been taught to stand stock-still and allow you to run along the rope, grab the calf, tie it up and administer the medicine. This procedure forms one of the competitions at all the big rodeos in the USA as well as in many parts of South America. As I say, the cowboys do it all in about ten seconds. It took me about ten hours to even catch my first calf. But it was fun and certainly a challenge. I did improve and it was important that I did, as it was a vital part of my job for the rest of the time I was in Argentina. I have never been called upon to use that skill ever again, so I cannot claim that it was a particularly important part of my education, nor in this sophisticated age, is it likely to be, but I still have my lasso and keep it oiled and ready for use – just in case!

One weekend a 'puestero', that is to say, a herdsman who lived in a small house on the estancia with his family away from the main headquarters, had his annual sausage-making fiesta. His whole family and many neighbours gathered at this puesto on Saturday afternoon and three big, fat pigs and one young horse were slaughtered. The meat from these was minced and mixed together; this mixture was then added to a delectable selection of spices and fed into ready prepared sausage skins. The resultant vast quantity of excellent sausages fed the family for a year.

The whole procedure took the entire weekend and was the excuse for a major party. There were plenty of spare pieces of meat that did not find their way into the sausages, and these were grilled and eaten over an open fire and washed down by quantities of cheap, but good, red wine. Guitars were produced and much dancing took place round the fire late into the night. Next day the slightly hung-over participants continued with the sausage-making – and wine drinking! I had been asked along and certainly contributed to the eating, drinking and even dancing but I do not think that the year's sausage production owed a lot to my presence.

It was one of the few occasions that one was able to get one's hands on the local talent. The puesteros all had large families and their teenage daughters tended to be very pretty. Dancing was a serious business and a competition to find the best pair of tango dancers was always a feature of any such occasion. I cannot claim to be much of a tango dancer, but after sufficient red wine I was prepared to give it a go and managed to persuade a young senorita to accompany me. I think she could have been quite good, but my limited skills were better suited to rock and roll, so the applause we got was more for 'effort' than artistic impression. I would say that my ensuing courtship with the senorita would have also gained many points for effort but, sadly, very few for actual achievement.

The only other 'skill' that I indulged in there was soccer. At school I had played little soccer, opting for rugger, cricket and hockey as my sports but in all of Argentina, soccer rules supreme and the village of Lopez Lecube was no exception. It boasted two teams, the best of which played in a local league. Matches were played on a Sunday afternoon on a dusty pitch behind the local pub – or bollichi, as it was called – and the whole village of some two hundred people turned out to cheer on their team.

I was fit and had played some soccer so volunteered to give it a go, egged on by Bob Skinner. I played in the second team, which usually had a game as a sort of curtain raiser to the main game. Despite a lot of noise, flamboyant gestures and many appeals to the referee the standard was not high; it can't have been, because, after a few games, I won promotion to the first team! I played centre forward and, in one never to be forgotten game, scored the winning goal against our big rivals, Sola, the neighbouring village. I had meant to try and head a corner kick but had slipped and the ball bounced off my shoulder completely wrong-footing the goalkeeper, and trickled over the goal line. It was a great mistake, as I was immediately mobbed by my teammates and even kissed by a lot of garlic smelling dagos. The match was so closely fought that three different referees had to be employed, the first two relinquishing the job when threatened with physical violence for penalising a player for a foul he, and all his teammates, thought he had not done. The opposition differed in this assessment and the first two referees were not prepared to argue their case. From then on I was a local hero – the 'gringo' who won the game for us against Sola . Luckily, this was virtually the last match of the season, so I was not called upon to maintain such an exalted status.

There were quite a lot of game birds on the farms, mainly a type of local partridge, and Bob Skinner lent me his ancient 12 bore and I had several amusing evenings wandering around having a go at these. Mrs. Skinner – Elva – came into her own here, as she pickled the plump little partridges and bottled them. A few months of maturing and the meat just fell off the bone and was quite delicious.

After about six months here I was ready to move on and, as no BA soccer club appeared to require my services, I asked the head office of Waldrons if I could go to one of their places up in the north of the country.

1
A Zimbo Gaucho

My final few months in Argentina were spent on an estancia in the far north of the country in the province of Corrientes where cattle ranching was the main occupation and the home of the much romanticised gaucho.

This part of Argentina, together with the provinces round BA, is the main cattle raising part of the country. The locals who live in Corrientes call themselves Corrientinos and are a very proud and fiery lot. Many are descended from the Guaranee Indians and the language of Guaranee is, or was then, still in general use. Luckily, Spanish was still the predominant language; as I was by now, becoming reasonably proficient at it and had no wish to try and speak a new, very obscure tongue.

The estancia was large and remote, being all of seventy miles from the nearest town or even village. Roads were bad at the best of times and completely impassable in a vehicle if there was any rain slightly above the average. I enjoyed my time there a lot as one worked with the real Argentinian gaucho. Every morning I caught one or two horses from the troop, which were driven into a corral. One, if I hoped to be back near the homestead by lunchtime, but more likely two, as one was usually too far away to come back for lunch, so took food along with you. Lunch, and indeed most meals, varied very little – quantities of raw meat and dry biscuits, called galleja. When setting off on a horse with this picnic you put the galleja in a saddlebag but tied the meat behind the saddle resting on the horse's back to get it nicely salted! One was allowed to eat as much meat as one wanted, but vegetables were very few and far between.

We were up and away as soon as the sun was up but had a long rest in the middle of the day when the salty meat was cooked over a wood fire. The drink was strong green tea which was put into a small gourd-like container called a mate`. To this was added boiling water and you sucked the resulting liquid out through a metal straw. It was refreshing and I became very fond of it. I did not, though, like the habit of passing the mate` and bombija round amongst a gathering of people and each in turn having a suck. You should have seen some of the bearded ruffians, with foul, tobacco scented breath, who had a suck and then passed it on to you to follow suit. It was considered very rude to refuse.

All my work mates wore long baggy trousers buttoned at the ankle, which were called bombachas. These were covered by canvas leggings and round the waist was wound a long sash out of which stuck a huge, lethal, very sharp knife, in a sheath, which also contained a sharpening iron, just to be sure that it always remained very sharp and lethal. The Corrientinos valued these knives highly and used them for virtually everything they did – skinning animals, cutting up their lunch, paring toenails, castrating sheep or calves, paring the dead skin from their feet or fighting. They were quick tempered and, after a few beers, tempers often flared and, if the argument became heated, out would come these knives and I witnessed at least two terrifying knife fights. The loser in each case sustained a terrible gash right down his cheek. I, too, carried a knife at all times but took good care not to get into any heated arguments.

The work was very similar to that at my last place so my newly found skill with the lasso came in very handy. Horses played a very prominent part in everybody's lives. The estancia owned the troop of workhorses, which were used every day, but each individual owned his own horse or horses, which, with the tacit agreement of the estancia owner, he kept handy. These were not used for daily work but kept for the weekend when they would be saddled up in some, usually fancy tack, and used to go visiting, courting, drinking or racing. Racing was very popular and took the form of challenge matches – "I bet my horse can beat yours over 500 metres," sort of thing. These challenge matches were taken very seriously and a lot of money wagered on them. The owner did not necessarily ride the horse himself in the race. He might be a large individual and carry too much weight, so an imported 'jockey' would be used. I met a number of these wizened little characters; they would arrive on the Saturday night, ready for the race, which always took part on the Sunday. They always had a lot to say and were much revered by the locals. Naturally, they were paid handsomely for their services both in cash and kind, for they were right royally entertained.

The race would be a gala occasion for all the estancia workers and many neighbours as well. It was a colourful scene with everyone dressed in his or her best, mounted on some lovely horseflesh. There were some very pretty girls who appeared at these events. They were wives and daughters of the labour force, all of whom lived permanently on the place. The pretty ones were usually the daughters. Argentinian women seem to mature young but run to fat and lose their looks quite soon! I never saw any of them on a horse, ever. They would be driven to occasions, such as the race, in a sulky and, once there, would not mix with the men at all but stood in a little group all on their own. Any advances that I tried to make were very quickly rebuffed, so, remembering those knives, I backed off quite speedily.

The actual race always started long after the advertised time and, once over, there would be endless objections from the loser with allegations of cheating, doping, nobbling, anything you like. No owner ever accepted defeat gracefully. If it were obvious that the horse had been well and truly beaten, the jockey was blamed and usually accused of ' pulling' the horse to stop it winning because he had money on the other one. I have never seen such a carry-on.

The race itself was never run over much more than 500 metres and the jockeys always rode bare back. The horses were mainly that wonderful, tough, little Argentinian breed, the Criollo, but sometimes there was a bit of English thoroughbred in there as well. The Criollo was the perfect cattle pony, usually not more than 15.3 hands high, very durable and extremely quick on its feet. It is therefore no coincidence that

Argentinian polo teams are the best in the world by some distance. Not only do the players have an enormous flair for the game, but they also have these magic ponies to play on.

There was no football on this estancia, I suppose because we were too remote and no village anywhere near, so the other main recreation, apart from the horse racing, was cards, and here I was introduced into the local game called 'trucu'. This was played with its own deck of cards and was really a kind of poker. Often on a Sunday, I would ride out to a small 'puesto' which was the home of the cattleman in charge of that part of the estancia. I would take along a skin of wine and they would provide the meat. This was either good beef steak or, a specialty of some, 'tripa gorda,' which is the fattest bit of the tripe turned inside out and grilled until it was crisp over a hot fire. The 'tripa gorda' cooked like this from a fat cow takes a lot of beating.

After the meal we would play trucu or toss the 'taba,' which is the knucklebone of a bull fitted with metal on each side. This has to be thrown into a sand pit and has to end up facing a certain direction. Some skill and a lot more betting. Each family had its own 'taba' and, before I left, one of them made a special one for me, which I still have. On these occasions the women folk of the family kept very much in the background again, it was certainly a pretty chauvinistic society.

I was there for six months and once asked if I could have a weekend off and go to town. The boss, Mr. Muntz, had no objection to this and said I could leave on Friday after lunch as long as I was back for work on Monday morning. The town, Curuzu Cuatia, was seventy miles away and there had been no offer of a vehicle to get me there, so I talked a friend into coming with me and we rode. There was nothing that unusual in doing this, people rode vast distances on horseback and the horses themselves had a special gait for these long journeys which was something between a trot and a canter. It covered the ground at about seven miles an hour and, sitting on the type of huge sheepskin saddle commonly used, one could almost nod off.

We took three horses each and rode until dark on that Friday afternoon, then hobbled the horses for the night and slept in the open. Next day we were in town by lunchtime and stabled the horses in some livery yards, then set out to see the town. There was not a lot to do in Curuzu Cuatia but it did have bars and dance halls. Here, the girls were a good deal more forthcoming than those on the estancia and my mate and I had the sort of Saturday night that we had hoped for. The price had to be paid next day, Sunday, when, after very little sleep and with a crashing hangover, we had to ride seventy miles back again.

I only took the one weekend off!

A highlight of the year was the catching and breaking of the three year old colts and fillies which had been running virtually wild on the estancia since birth. Their only previous contact with human beings was when they had been caught and branded as yearlings and, in the case of the colts, castrated. Certainly, they had never been handled at all and had to be driven into a large, strong corral like a herd of wild cattle. This was an exciting exercise as, when the youngsters saw us coming, they ran away, probably remembering what had happened to them last time they had been caught! They were young and fit and did not have to carry anyone on their back and so could go faster than us. A lot of hard riding over rough country, a certain amount of cunning and quite a lot of luck resulted in us getting most of them into the corral by about eight o' clock.

Once there, each member of the workforce was entitled to choose one potro, as they were called, for his own use in the years to come. He had to catch it, halter train it and be riding it by nightfall! The catching was the first dramatic bit. All the frightened youngsters would be bunched together in a corner of the corral, then a delegated rider would try and single one out and drive it, at full gallop, through a narrow gate which led into an adjoining corral. Standing beside the gateway would be the guy who wanted to catch and train that particular horse. As the horse thundered through the gate he would snake out his lasso and catch its front feet. Both of them. Needless to say this

43

caused the wretched animal to crash to the ground and, while it lay stunned, its new trainer would rush up to it and put on a very strong rawhide halter. He would then enlist the help of a few other guys and, as the horse got up, drag it to a stout pole on the edge of the corral and attach it firmly.

Thus, this totally wild, young, strong horse, which had virtually never even seen a human being at close range, was anchored to a pole with people and noise all round it. Obviously, it was terrified and fought like mad against the halter, pulling backwards, leaping forwards and often falling over. If it showed signs of getting tired and slackening off its endeavour to get free, it would be beaten and made to fight some more.

There were some twelve potros caught this way and tied up, each with its potential new owner in attendance. Rather foolhardily, I asked if I could have one to train as well, while I was still at the estancia. My request was granted with enthusiasm as there were still half a dozen young horses so far uncaught, and the idea of watching the gringo make a fool of himself, appealed to the assembled workers.

A strong looking bay gelding was selected for me and I stood nervously by the gate while it was driven flat out towards me. As it flashed through the gate, I threw out my lasso in a sort of vertical hoop with the bottom of the rope on the ground and the top about knee high. The horse's legs hit the top rope and I hauled back pulling the lasso tight. Got him! I ran forward and sat on his head to prevent him getting up, as he lay struggling in the dust. Help was forthcoming and we soon had my potro safely tied up alongside the others.

Honour was at stake. It was mid-morning by now, so I only had a few hours to convince this wild colt that it would be a good idea for him to let me sit on his back. As he snorted in terror and flung himself backwards, straining against the halter, whenever I came within ten yards of him, this seemed highly unlikely. I stole a quick look at how my fellow workers were faring and what they were doing. It appeared to be very much a carrot and stick performance. First they would encourage their animal to fight against the halter to tire itself out and then, when it was obviously distressed, they would approach its head and try to rub it behind the ears or stroke its muzzle. This stroking would progress down the neck, onto the withers and eventually under the chest and belly. All the time they would be talking softly to the animal.

I tried doing the same and by about three o' clock, he would stand stock still with all four legs well spread and, although quivering all over, allow me to stroke him. What now? A small, folded blanket was then thrown over the back. More stroking, then this was followed by a surcingle, which was gingerly fastened round his girth and very gradually tightened. I noticed that on top of the surcingle, a sort of loop or handhold had been sewn. I was lent one of these and put it round my guy. It was four-thirty.

Down the line from me, there was increasing activity and suddenly I saw one of the horses being untied and a rider with one hand on the halter and the other on the loop of the surcingle. Two other mounted riders on trained horses stood nearby. As the horse was released the rider vaulted onto its back and at the same time the two hovering horsemen moved in on either side of the young horse. All hell was then let loose. With a fart and a buck the young horse took off, very closely followed by the other two who positioned themselves on either side of the youngster. This threesome then sped off into the middle distance with the rider of the young horse beating it with his revenke and the two outriders sort of steering it. The object of this exercise, I was told, was to tire the youngster so much that it finally stopped, exhausted and accepted its new rider – that is if he was still there!

Not all were. Horses, like anything else, vary considerably and the stronger, more spirited ones often proved too much for their rider and, despite the attentions of the two outriders, would deposit him unceremoniously in a heap on the ground. This would be greeted by loud jeers from anyone fortunate enough to be nearby.

Time was getting on and most of the others had disappeared in a cloud of dust. I attracted the attention of two mounted riders and indicated that I was ready to go for a gentle hack and would they like to come along as well. Not being as agile as some of my fellows, I decided not to vault straight on, but to lie over my horse's back and then swing my right leg over when I felt secure. Well, I never got a chance to feel remotely secure. As my chest touched his back he skewed sideways and I landed flat on my back in the dust. Much mirth from my riding companions and shouted advice to get on properly or the same thing would happen again. So I leapt and, probably because the horse moved at just the right time, I landed squarely on the blanket on his back. My left hand still held the end of the halter and with my right I held on to the loop on the surcingle as though my life depended on it – it probably did, as the three of us shot off at an alarming speed out of the corral and flat out across the pampas. "Beat him, beat him," urged my companions. This would have meant taking my hand off the surcingle loop and I was very disinclined to do this, but it did not really matter as my companions started beating my horse for me. This produced predictable results – we went even faster, so fast though, that the horse did not really have time to buck, so I was able to cling on, close my eyes and pray.

I do not know how far we went. I did not have my passport with me so we must have stopped somewhere before the Paraguay border, but suddenly we did slow down and eventually ground to a halt. My poor little horse was completely blown and stood with its head down and sides heaving. Its poor little rider was not much better off. My companions did not allow us long to rest, but turned us round and we headed back to the homestead. As dusk was falling we walked quite sedately into the corral we had left some thirty minutes before and I dismounted, took off the surcingle and led my horse to water – the first he had had that day.

There are better and kinder ways of breaking a horse in, but they take longer. This is the way the Argies did it on the cattle estancias in the 1950s and probably still do as far as I know. I called my horse 'Mercury' and rode him regularly until I left some three months later. There was something special in reasoning that I was the only person who had ever sat on his back.

One day, riding back from work at about six in the evening I spotted a man standing under a tree. No horse was visible, which was odd, as I was still some distance from the homestead and everyone went everywhere on horseback. I approached him to see if he had fallen off and his horse had run away. Again, this was unlikely as all the horses are trained to stand still once their rider dismounts. He just drops the reins, which are not joined as in England, so they fall to the ground and the horse will not move so long as these reins lie on the ground in front of it. The man did not answer my first call so I rode closer and it was only then that I realised his feet were not actually touching the ground.

He was hanging by his neck from one of the branches and was stone dead.

He turned out to be a schoolmaster from one of the very basic, little local schools dotted round in the area. We duly reported the matter to the local police who took a very relaxed view on the whole thing and I actually ended up writing the police report as the constable, who eventually came out to investigate, was barely literate. As my Spanish was also barely literate, the report will have made interesting reading.

My days in Corrientes ended in a social whirl! I had not enjoyed much of that sort of thing during my stay in Argentina, so it all came as a bit of a surprise. December was show time in Concordia, the capital of Corrientes, and the whole Muntz family departed to that city for a week to attend the show. I was left behind, but told that I could join them when I had completed a couple of outstanding jobs. They even said that I could come to Concordia in the ancient farm Chevvy truck – or camionetta, as they were called. This was a rare privilege, but I was not about to ride the two hundred miles to the show!

Jobs completed, I set off down the dirt road and made slow, but steady progress to the attractive little farming town of Concordia. Show week was the main event of the year, both business wise and social. After the judging and awarding of prizes, most of the livestock was auctioned and sold. Mr. Muntz bought some Romney Marsh rams and I had to keep an eye on these while I was there. Every evening there was a gala dance held at one of the four or five hotels. There were a lot of other people in town and I met up with a bunch of guys of my own age who worked on neighbouring estancias and were basically English, or at least English speaking. Some had actually come out from England and were doing the same sort of thing as I, so we were a happy little gang of about eight or ten. One of them was still at Cambridge University, where, perhaps, I should have been. His college was Trinity and he had a little limerick, which went as follows:

> There was a young fellow from Trinity,
> Who ruined his sister's virginity,
> He stole from his mother,
> Buggered his brother,
> Then got a first in Divinity.

Dances started every night at about ten o' clock and never ended before dawn. I went to four in succession and was never in bed before six-thirty. Fortunately, there appeared to be a number of quite pretty girls, relatively unattached. Some were English, but most Argentinian and, as they came from the town, were a bit more receptive to our advances than those back on the estancias. Our gang embarked on a charm offensive! I met and made some progress with three different girls. All were Argentinian and all called Mercedes!! Seems it was a popular name in Concordia some twenty years ago. They spoke a little English but mostly Spanish at which, by this time, I rather fancied myself.

One night, or early one morning, we all took a boat across the River Plate to a town called Salto on the opposite bank and it was only next day that I learned that Salto was actually in Paraguay, the river being the international boundary.

Going to bed so late and being involved with so many Mercedes, meant that Mr. Muntz's rams had to more or less fend for themselves, but they seemed to survive OK and it was a pretty weary driver who finally took them back to El Chania.

Very soon after this I finally left. The rains had broken in no uncertain fashion and as the date that I was due to leave approached I began to wonder how I was going to get off the estancia. The roads were pretty much impassable and all the rivers very high. It was going to be a problem and I had to be back in BA to catch a boat leaving for Cape Town.

In the event we had to charter a small 'plane to fly me to Curuzu. This landed on a sort of flat bit of ground about a mile from the homestead and I, together with a few others, rode out to it carrying my baggage between us. Having boarded and bid fond farewells all round, it was soon apparent that the 'plane was stuck in the wet ground. Everyone dismounted and proceeded to push. With much spinning of wheels and shouts from the pilot we eventually got going and were soon airborne.

My day's adventures were far from over. Arriving in Curuzu I got to the station to discover that the only train that would connect with my train to BA had already left and I had to hitch a lift on, what turned out to be a sewage truck, to the next station and just managed to catch the train there. From there we went to Parana`, and on to a launch down the River Plate to Santa Fe, followed by an overnight train to BA where I arrived at ten o' clock the next morning. In the previous twenty-four hours I had experienced a variety of transport – an aeroplane, boat, two trains, three taxis, a horse and a sewage truck!

As it turned out the big rush was unnecessary as my ship had been delayed and I had to remain in BA for another ten days. This coincided with Christmas 1959. Luckily some of the friends that I had made on my travels were in BA and they looked after me very well and I spent Christmas Day with John Wilson and his family. Most of the big estancia owners in Argentina did not live on them. They preferred to live in luxury in BA and hire a manager, only visiting the place for a month or so every year. I think that Peron had tried to change this as he pretended to champion the cause of the poor, but clearly he had failed as there were plenty of very rich owners and the poor remained pretty poor. Perhaps if he had told them to invade the estancias and take them over, as Robert Mugabe did in Zimbabwe forty-five years later, he would have remained in power a little longer than he did, instead of being ousted for the corrupt dictator that he was and forced to live in exile in Spain.

I finally left Argentina on the last day of 1959 and sailed down the River Plate on the Royal Interocean line's M.V. Tegelburg and arrived back in Africa two weeks later. Two weeks!! Imagine taking that long to get from BA to Cape Town these days.

Had I enjoyed my eighteen months in Argentina and had it done me any good? I suppose that both are partly true. These days youngsters of the age I was then do the same sort of thing but not for so long a stretch in one place. It would have been more fun if I had gone with a mate, I was very lonely at times, particularly early on when my Spanish was non-existent and I seldom knew what was going on. I am no linguist and although I was fairly fluent, in a pretty rough sort of way, by the time I left, I have forgotten it all now. I learned a few unlikely skills, none of which have been much use to me since, although the amount of riding I did probably contributed to the enjoyment I have had out of horses ever since.

9
Harry

It takes 15 minutes to get from Leeds farmhouse to my house at Chirume in Zimbabwe but on the day of the fire I did do it in 12 minutes, but then the car was never quite the same ever again! The night we were attacked by Mugabe's thugs and just managed to get a distress call out on the farm radio, Harry did the trip in seven minutes.

But then Harry was like that; he was always first on the scene if there was trouble brewing and last to leave. And there was plenty of trouble on white-owned Zimbabwe farms in the early years of this century. Having just lost a referendum for the first time in his 20 year 'reign', Mugabe was determined to win the imminent general election and, to this end, had enlisted the services of his supporters who had actually fought in the 'Bush War' that had led to Independence from Britain. A number of genuine 'war veterans' in many farming areas, were told to gather together a band of thugs and terrorize the resident farmers into abandoning their farms. The fact that most of this gang had barely been born when the war ended did not matter as they were paid to do their job and fed alcohol and drugs to aid any inhibitions about doing it!

While it was policy to try and get all farmers off the land, a tried and trusted method of singling out a particular target and really making an example of it was adopted, in that in most farming areas one farmer was selected and either killed or very badly beaten up. The theory being; 'Kill one, scare a thousand'. Harry could well have been that target in the Wedza area.

Having completed a four year degree course in Agricultural Economics and passed out as top student at the University of New England in Australia, Harry was offered many lucrative jobs in that progressive country, but no, all he wanted to do was farm in his native Zimbabwe, so he returned to Africa and initially worked for a bank in Harare before marrying Flip and fulfilling his ambition by taking over Leeds farm in the Wedza farming area.

Not all top students are necessarily much good at the practical side of farming, but, far from pretending that he knew it all, Harry enlisted the help of his well-established neighbours and was very soon producing some very good crops indeed. Caspar, his son, was soon born on the farm and everything in the garden was rosy.

Then came the referendum, and Mugabe's ZANU [PF] party was soundly defeated for the first time in 20 years of autocratic rule. A terrified Mugabe suddenly realised that there was a distinct possibility that he could be voted out of power at the next election, due in a few short months' time. It was therefore time for some drastic measures.

And drastic measures they were. Land has always been an emotive issue in Africa so Mugabe focused on this. He hired gangs of thugs [which he erroneously called "War Veterans"] and sent them to the scattered, isolated farmhouses throughout Zimbabwe to harass the farmer and his family and demand that the farm be handed over to them.

The severity of this harassment varied from area to area and our area, Wedza, was one of the worst. Leader of the thugs in Wedza was a guy who actually had been in the liberation struggle, as it is now called. His name was Fanuel Chigwadere and he crossed swords with Harry at a very early stage.

All farmers in Wedza were in more or less permanent contact with each other by means of a high band radio system, so, if anyone was in particular trouble, they put out a plea for help and anyone in the vicinity dropped everything they were doing and went. This was important because the police had been told not to react to any distress calls from white farmers. Indeed, when farmers in the Mrewa district actually drove to their local police station because they were being shot at, they were turned away and handed over to the very thugs from whom they were seeking legal protection. This resulted in one being murdered and five beaten up and left for dead.

When a call for help went out in the Wedza area, Harry was invariably the first one to arrive. Invariably, also, the leader of the problem would be Chigwadere, surrounded by a bunch of young thugs either drunk or high on drugs. In truth, there was not a great deal that Harry, or anyone else, could do except provide moral support to the wretched farmer who would be barricaded into his house, by letting him know by radio that at least there was someone on his side in the vicinity. Harry would do this and he would also be what nuisance he could possibly be to Chigwadere and his thugs. Again, this was very little and really amounted to little more than letting the air out of their tyres, but this sort of thing did annoy Chigwadere intensely. On one occasion Harry took along some of his own labour to give the impression that he was backed up by numbers. Miraculously, on this occasion the police suddenly appeared on the scene. Did they arrest Chigwadere for illegally harassing an innocent farmer? Not a bit of it, they arrested Harry – for "disturbing the peace".

This was scary as there was no way of knowing what would happen to him once in the hands of the police. In the event he appeared in court (the first of many such visits!) and was released on bail. This did not please Chigwadere, who now enlisted the services of a particularly nasty bunch of young thugs from an African owned farm near Leeds to put as much pressure as they could on Harry. The head of this bunch was called Dauga, a young black farmer who Harry had gone out of his way to help by supplying him with seedlings and giving him advice on his crops.

Dauga and his mates were paid a daily wage by the government to do their job. They cut the fences on Leeds, they set fire to the grass, they stole cattle, they planted token plots of maize on Leeds and then drove Harry's cattle into the seedlings as they came up, and then claimed massive compensation for the damage done. When Harry refused to pay, they barricaded him, Flip and Caspar into their house and cut off the water supply. They ripped the plastic covers off Harry's paprika seedlings and dug up the seedbeds. They tried to get his own labour to call him out of his house at night for some supposed urgent problem, while they waited in ambush, armed with gum poles, ready to beat him when he appeared and then disappear under cover of darkness. They dragged logs across his drive and even put a wire fence across with a guard on it claiming that Harry had no right to pass [to his own house!]. They made the life of his labour force a complete misery and frequently beat them up.

All this, Harry religiously reported to the police, but they never came out to help, always claiming lack of transport, busy on another case or just plain lies, saying they were coming, with no intention of doing so. But Harry wrote it all down and even recorded the names of the policemen who said they were coming.

Let it be quite clear that in the eyes of the law in Zimbabwe at that time, Harry was the 100% legal owner of the farm and it was the duty of the police to protect him against just the sort of things that were happening.

Come the presidential elections in 2002 Harry volunteered to escort monitors of the opposition party to polling stations in the Wedza area. This is a job that should have been a) unnecessary or b) done by the police. Harry literally took his life in his hands to escort legally accredited monitors to remote rural polling stations. Once there, he had to drop these brave men under cover of darkness, then make his own lonely way home before picking them up again next morning. Some, he could not find, they had been spotted and disappeared into the bush and so were unable to give their version of "the free and fair election".

Chigwadere heard that Harry was doing this and set up road blocks to catch him, [surely only police can set up road blocks?] and when he failed, he notified the police that Harry [and others] had been transgressing the rules of the election by venturing illegally near to polling booths. The police agreed and came to arrest Harry. But Harry was getting smart by now and had "gone on holiday".

Chigwadere vowed that if ZANU [PF] won the election he would have Harry off his farm within 48 hours [this, despite Harry having a High Court order saying he was legally entitled to carry on farming]. ZANU [PF] did win the election – of course they did, the opposition party was not given time to vote in the urban areas, those in rural areas were too terrified not to vote for them and unsupervised voting boxes were stuffed full of rigged voting papers.

Harry decided it was time for a holiday in Mozambique and quietly disappeared. Chigwadere duly appeared on Leeds breathing fire and brimstone to find no one there. But Harry came back from Mozambique. There was not a lot he could do farming wise as all his seedbeds had been destroyed, but he still had his cattle. He had some 350 head in all but by the time he finally moved them off the farm there were just over 50 – all the rest had been stolen.

About this time the government decided that the judiciary was a bit too honest, so they sacked most of the longstanding, experienced, unbiased judges and replaced them with their own men. Even these men were hard pressed to find a legal reason for kicking Harry off his farm. He qualified in every respect, as the type of farmer that the newly re-elected president said would be allowed to remain on his farm. Nevertheless, they did give him a deadline by which time he had to be off. Harry steadfastly refused to move. The courts had ruled that the farm was still his, so why should he go? Most of the rest of Wedza had by now abandoned their farms and were vainly trying to get off what possessions they could. The police issued a warrant for Harry's arrest.

Other people had warrants out for their arrest and there was much debate as to how best to cope with this – go into hiding or hand oneself in – the short answer was that you were bound to be found sooner or later and your evasiveness would count against you so why not just get it over with? Harry handed himself over and duly appeared in court charged with contravening some trumped-up charge that he was illegally living in his own house. In the sort of parody of justice that prevailed in Zimbabwe at that time, Harry was released on bail, but told he could not return to his home. All this, despite High Court orders saying that he was still the legal owner of his farm.

There was really not much option, he had to leave or be locked up. On the farm were still all his cattle, tonnes of fertiliser and crop chemicals ready for the new season's crop, all his farm equipment and most of his personal belongings. Also, of course, his remaining loyal labour force.

With bad grace, Harry moved to Harare but mounted a campaign through the courts to get the resident squatters on his farm evicted. As there was an existing order saying the farm was still his, no court with any pretence of legality could not order the squatters [or 'new settlers,' as they liked to be known] to leave. So Harry won his case. He moved back on to the farm.

Armed with this new court order he drove out to Wedza and confronted the District Administrator, the member in charge of the police and the "war veteran" leader, Chigwadere. All were hard to find and, when eventually cornered were very reluctant to speak to Harry, let alone accept the papers. Chigwadere was the hardest to find but eventually Harry spotted him walking down Wedza's main road while he was talking to the police chief Chitzanzaro. Harry immediately broke away from this conversation and strode up to his arch enemy, put his arm round his shoulder and said, "Fanuel! How lovely to see you." Chigwadere nearly exploded. So, while he was in a state of total confusion, Harry pressed the court order into his hands and started explaining what it was all about. I think the word is incandescent with fury, if it is, Chigwadere was certainly that. He wrenched himself free and strode off down the road ripping the court order to shreds and throwing it over his shoulder as he went.

Harry gently pointed out to the police officer that he was destroying an official document with which he was meant to comply.

There was never any chance of that; far from leaving the farm, the squatters exerted more pressure on Harry and his family with the [only just] covert support of the police.

On one occasion a group of thugs had surrounded one of Harry's tractors and were threatening to burn it. Harry was warned and phoned the police. They claimed to have no transport and refused to come and help. With absolutely no official backing there was nothing Harry could do. He watched helplessly as the thugs blatantly stole his fertiliser but when they did start trying to burn the tractor, who should step out from behind a bush but the police member-in-charge from Wedza. He had been there all the time and was quite happy to watch the fertiliser being stolen, but, not knowing that Harry was watching, decided that actually burning the tractor was a waste, and told the thugs to desist.

Shortly after this Harry moved a lot of his remaining equipment to my farm for safekeeping. When Chigwadere paid me a visit he spotted the tractor and told me to tell Harry that he wanted to hire it and would pay 'up front' for the use of it. Harry was fairly short of money as, not only was he being prevented from farming, but was losing many of his capital assets hand over fist. I put Chigwadere's proposal to him.

The response was explosive, "No way will I help people who are stealing my farm, and I would rather see the thing burned." Later it was.

Chigwadere may have been Harry's worst enemy but there is no doubt that he secretly admired him! Indeed once when one of Mugabe's high ranking Central Intelligence Officers was causing trouble at the butchery on Leeds farm, Harry was spotted writing down the man's car number. Furious about this, the Officer wanted to arrest Harry and take him back to Harare with him for 'questioning'. It was then that Chigwadere, who was accompanying this high ranking official, stepped in and told him to lay off Harry.

One of the thugs who was occupying Harry's farm was actually a policeman called Mano. He had been 'given' a bit of land and, like many others, had planted a token crop of maize with no fertiliser and no fence to protect it. Soon there were a few stunted, little yellow plants peeping through the arid soil with absolutely no hope of ever producing any sort of cobs. These were soon eaten by duiker or kudu, which at that time still roamed free on the farm.

The policeman/new farmer immediately appeared on Harry's doorstep demanding compensation for the loss of his crop which, he said, had been eaten by Harry's cattle.

Needless to say Harry just laughed at him. The reaction was swift. All the other squatters claimed similar grievances and converged on the homestead. Harry, Flip, Caspar and little Lucy, who, although based in Harare now, happened to be out at the farm, were barricaded into their house and the water cut off.

I drove over to see what help I could be. I sat in my truck outside the locked gates into Harry's house. The leader of the thugs had put his own padlock on the gate and would not let me in to speak to Harry. I tried to convince them that the only fair way to resolve the situation was for a neutral assessor to come and view the damage and decide what compensation should be paid. It was all I could think of but it never got past first base. The thugs would not accept it as obviously there was precious little to assess and, when I eventually did manage to talk to Harry on the radio, he would not accept it either, as he said, correctly, that the whole thing was a set-up and he would not be party to any bogus settlement.

I cannot remember how it all ended. They were locked in for a good two days, then Flip and the children were allowed to go and, finally, Harry managed to get out under cover of darkness.

Meanwhile, his cattle were being quite openly driven off the farm and, quite clearly the police were heavily involved. Harry was taking notes all the time and eventually had enough evidence to bring a case of theft against the police. He approached the police chiefs in Marondera and Harare and enlisted the services of a Harare lawyer. Promises were made, investigations were to follow, more papers were required and so it went on and on but nothing was actually done.

Shortly after, I was playing golf in Marondera with Harry when his mobile phone suddenly went. It was the police in Wedza; they wanted him to report to them immediately. Wedza is 35 miles from Marondera and 120 from Harare, where Harry was then living, and it was already four-forty in the afternoon. Harry asked what was so urgent and was told that he was under arrest on three counts

1] Carrying a pistol without a valid permit.

2] Contravening the new P O S A law, [Public Order Security Act] in that he had said the policemen investigating his case would lose their jobs when this government was kicked out of power.

3] And, more sinister, for threatening a member of the police force with a firearm.

Harry asked when all this was supposed to have happened. It seemed that it was some three days before when Harry was trying to do a follow-up on some of his stolen cattle. Threatening the police with a firearm is a very serious offence. Why then had he not been arrested there and then? Why had they waited three days to charge him? Harry denied all charges but said he would report to the Wedza police station on the morrow. He then switched off his phone and completed his round of golf as if nothing were wrong and actually won the tournament.

I insisted on going with Harry to Wedza next morning. He did not want me to, insisting that there was no case to answer and it was all just designed to annoy him. Nevertheless he was dressed in jeans and rugby jersey and was armed with mosquito repellent and sleeping pills – a clear indication that he thought he was likely to be locked up and wanted to be prepared.

I thought otherwise. To me it was a set-up by the police because they knew that Harry had a watertight case against them.

This proved to be the case. The policeman who questioned Harry, Constable Mano, and then took his statement, was one of the very policemen who were involved in the abortive quest for stolen cattle when the so-called incidents had occurred. He insisted on pressing all three charges, despite the fact that Harry showed him his valid firearm certificate and reminded him that, far from threatening him with a gun, he had, in fact, handed the firearm over to him voluntarily. The whole process dragged on and on, then, just as we were about to leave with a promise to appear in court next day, the member-in-charge, Inspector Chitzanzaro, arrived on the scene and told Harry to follow him into his office. Chitzanzaro hated Harry's guts and was almost certainly involved in the theft of his cattle himself. I was not allowed to follow. I spent an anxious half-hour wondering what was happening in that office. Harry finally emerged with a wry grin on his face. It transpired that as he entered the office, Chitzanzaro had snapped at the constable accompanying Harry, "Take him to the cells". If I had not been there I think they would have locked him up there and then. Or it may just have been bluff to frighten Harry, but Harry does not frighten easily.

Next day Harry engaged the services of the local black lawyer, Richard Mufuka, and they had little difficulty in getting the case remanded with Harry out of custody, but paying a hefty bail.

I thought that this might have dampened Harry's ardour over trying to prosecute a corrupt police force, but, not a bit of it, he went at it with more vigour than ever. It was now too dangerous to go out to his farm at all, as, clearly the police would offer him no protection and the resident thugs all knew this. Of his original herd of some 350 head he managed to rescue a paltry 50 cows, the rest were stolen, as was all his fertiliser and most of his equipment. His house was trashed and all the fencing removed.

Harry now had no income, no job, no home and had lost most of his capital assets. He also had a wife and two small children to support. A friend quite near where we had settled ourselves after being evicted from our home and farm lent him a cottage.

I continued to play golf with Harry from time to time and it soon became evident that there was nothing left for him in Zimbabwe but he could not leave the country, as he had had to surrender his passport as part of his bail conditions.

He was always cheerful and kept himself busy by annoying the police top brass in both Marondera and Harare by pushing them to investigate the corruption going on in the Wedza police force. They always pretended to be very concerned and interested but absolutely nothing ever happened. Every month or so Harry had to appear back in court to face the ridiculous charges. It seemed that the prosecution was never able to come up with its witnesses and the case was always remanded.

Finally Harry had had enough and applied for a job in Tanzania. This he got and went to the police to ask for his passport back. He had appeared in court whenever asked to and they had failed to produce witnesses, now he wanted to start working again in another country as, clearly, Zimbabwe did not want him. I think they were glad to be rid of him, because they gave him the passport back on condition that he returned for one last court appearance in six months' time.

He came to see me the day before he finally left Zimbabwe – and all his dreams.

"Good-bye, Father," he said. I forgot to mention earlier that Harry is my son.

8
Daniel's Dream

Daniel was only six when his mother died so his father had to look after him and his father was not a rich man. Faison, Daniel's father, worked as a gardener for a rich white man on a huge farm in Zimbabwe. Daniel did not know the white man's name as his father just referred to him as 'The Boss'.

The Boss was not a bad man and paid Faison a regular wage and provided him and Daniel with a small thatched hut to live in. It was not very smart and had no running water or even proper windows. It was located in a fenced off area known as 'The Compound'. Here there were many other similar houses in which lived nearly a hundred other workers on The Boss's farm.

These other workers went off every day except Sunday to work in the tobacco fields; tobacco being the main crop grown on the farm. Daniel went off every morning too and sat by his father in The Boss's garden while Faison planted out seedlings, weeded the vegetable garden or mowed the lawn. It was not very exciting and as Daniel sat there he gazed up at The Boss's house. It was huge! Great big gleaming windows provided glimpses of what went on inside. There was polished furniture, tables with shiny things on, pictures on the walls, comfortable chairs and wonderful soft beds. From the kitchen came delicious smells and occasionally his father would be given a morsel of food from this heaven by the cook, who was a friend, and did sometimes 'liberate' a small something which The Boss's wife never even noticed.

What would it be like to live in a house like that? wondered little Daniel. Once he mentioned it to his father who just laughed. "You silly little boy" he said, "How could we ever afford that sort of thing?" However, as he sat on the lawn while his father worked, Daniel did dream that one day he would live in a house like that, have servants of his own, sleep in a comfortable bed, eat good food three times a day and even own a car ! Wow! He hadn't thought of that.

The years slipped by. Daniel was educated at the farm school and when he was seventeen, he got a job of his own on the farm and joined the other workers in the tobacco lands. He did not go up to The Boss's house much now but often saw him when he came to supervise the work in a smart new Land Rover or driving off the farm with his wife in an even smarter Mercedes car. What an easy, wonderful life he leads as a farmer, thought Daniel.

Then there was an election in the country and it looked as though the long-time ruler of the country would lose for the first time in twenty years. Daniel had not thought much about politics up until now but suddenly everyone was talking about who would rule the country next. Angry men wearing dark glasses came out from Harare and told all the workers on the farm that if they did not vote for the current ruler and his party they would certainly be in for a lot of trouble. They said that if they did as they were told they would all be given land and a better standard of living. But the first thing to be done was to chase out the white men who had "stolen" their land when the country became a colony of Britain.

This was exciting talk and Daniel listened very attentively. What a good idea, he thought. So when more men came out from Harare saying that they were going to chase out The Boss, he willingly joined the gang that rampaged up to the house, broke down the gate at the entrance and started throwing stones through the windows and demanding that The Boss leave and go back to England. Daniel felt a little bit sorry for The Boss who had always paid his labour force the correct amount of money every month and provided the school he had been to and sponsored the football team and a few other things – but so should he, he could afford it. The thought of getting all the things that the men from Harare promised was heady stuff.

This thought grew and grew in Daniel's mind until he became so keen on the ideas that he became something of a leader among the gang of young men that now terrorised the whole area demanding that the white bosses vacate their farms and hand them over to the indigenous blacks. His enthusiasm was noticed by the men from Harare and Daniel was even paid some money to recruit more young men to his gang and told which farms to go to and how best to get the white owners to leave.

Things were getting very exciting with the whole country in uproar but his own boss still stubbornly refused to leave his house. Finally, Daniel was ordered to take his gang, go to The Boss's house, beat him up and tell him if he did not leave he would be killed. Daniel drank a large amount of cheap vodka which was supplied by the men from Harare and went to the house – the huge, smart house whose windows he had gazed through as a child. The Boss was there on his own as his wife now lived in Harare because of all the violence and they had to break down the front door to reach him. They caught him and beat him until he was only half conscious.

Daniel then leaned over him and said, "I once had a dream that I would live in a house like this and now I will because you are leaving." The Boss looked at Daniel through bloodshot eyes and spoke through swollen lips, "OK, little garden boy's son who I have always looked after, I will leave now but I also have a dream. One day this madness will end and I will return to the house and farm that I bought with hard-earned money and people like you will be brought to justice."

Daniel just laughed, kicked The Boss in the ribs and, with the help of others, dragged him out to the Mercedes telling him to leave and never return. In triumph Daniel then moved into the house, as was his right as leader of the gang.

A little later the current ruler and his party won the election and as a reward for what he had done, Daniel was awarded the whole farm and the house. "So dreams do come true," he said to his old and frail father, "would you like to come and live in my guest room?" he added with a laugh.

The years slipped by and Daniel grew fat and lazy. It had all been quite fun to begin with. He had sold some of The Boss's cattle whenever he needed money, then he had hired out the tractors and trailers to carry people into town, then he had chopped down the trees and sold the wood but soon there was nothing much left to sell and he applied to the same government that was still in power for a loan so that he could go on farming. They promised him all sorts of things and did send him some sacks of flour to feed his staff but this had not been grown in Zimbabwe. Rooms in the lovely smart house had been rented out to provide much needed income but the whole place was desperately rundown. Perhaps farming was not quite as easy as he had thought.

Then there was another election and the old government that Daniel had supported lost. A new and honest government took over and one day a slightly shabby Mercedes drew up in front of 'Daniel's house'. It was followed by a number of other vehicles some of which were police cars. An old man got stiffly out of the Mercedes and walked slowly towards the house. Daniel, looking unshaven and slightly hung-over, slouched in a battered armchair as the old man and his followers came into the sitting room.

"Good morning, little garden boy's son," said the old man, "I have come to reclaim my house and my farm. It is too late for me to reclaim all the cattle that you stole or the tractors that you have ruined but these men here have come to arrest you and you will be charged on several counts of causing grievous bodily harm, theft and treason."

The old man then turned round and held out his hand to an old lady. "Come along, darling," he said, "Dreams do come true, we are back in our home at last but there is an awful lot of work to do."

5
African Finance

"But your credit rating is appalling, Comrade, I cannot just hand over two million United States dollars to you with absolutely no security whatsoever. I want to help but even I would have to explain such a large unsecured loan to my Cabinet." The president of East Guinnea was sitting at the coffee table on the veranda of State House on the shores of the Atlantic Ocean. Opposite him was an agitated looking president of Zimbia sipping spasmodically at a cup of coffee which must have gone cold long ago.

"My health is poor and I urgently need to visit my doctors in Malaysia. The vindictive capitalists in London have deliberately sabotaged my country's last remaining long-haul aircraft and right at the moment we do not have the funds to pay engineers to rectify the faults. It managed to limp home but is now grounded at our international airport. You have brought me here on your own private jet to discuss other matters but when I return to Harata tomorrow I must proceed to Kuala Lumpa as soon as possible but I do not have the means of getting there." The long-standing president of Zimbia just hated admitting that his country no longer had even one aircraft working which could take him to see his doctors.

"Surely it would not cost $2 million to get your 'plane flying again, would it, Comrade?" stalled the president of East Guinnea.

"Unfortunately there are still some unpaid arrears due to these engineers and I am told by my Minister of Transport that they will not entertain any further repairs until their account is paid in full. These people seem to forget what I did for them in the liberation struggle, there is no patriotism, they are ungrateful swines but I tell you, Comrade...," He was cut short by a peremptory wave of the hand from his host who stood up saying,

"Debts still have to be paid though, my friend. Now, if I do lend you this money – and I say if – is there any sort of guarantee that I will ever get my money back?"

"I confess to you that I am so desperate that I will give you my personal cheque, drawn on a Swiss bank of some repute, and post-dated 30 days from now. If my government has not repaid you by then you may cash it."

The president of East Guinnea chuckled and said, "These cheques are easily stopped but I will lend you the money and if it is not repaid within 30 days – no more oil. And I mean NO MORE OIL. Your government is already considerably in – what was the word you used? Areas, arrears? Whatever – you already owe me a lot of money."

"You mean that my government owes your government certain slightly overdue funds."

"Yes, yes, yes we do understand each other. Do you agree to these terms?"

"If you can transfer two million United States dollars to this account, I will guarantee that it will be refunded in full within 30 days," said the flustered president of Zimbia, handing over a piece of paper to his host.

"Plus interest at the rate of 10% for the month, making a total of US$2,200,000," chuckled the president of East Guinnea, knowing that he had his guest over a barrel and seeing no reason why he should not make a quiet profit for himself – to go with several other 'quiet profits'.

"If you insist, Comrade, if you insist but I did think that you would waive any interest charges when one remembers the help my army gave you over that attempted coup."

"That debt has been repaid many times over – not least in the way that we continue to supply you with oil despite the afore-mentioned arrears."

So the deal was struck and a chastened president of Zimbia accepted a lift home in his host's private jet but was pleased to find that the promised two million was already in the stipulated account when he telephoned his friend, the Minister of Finance, to find out.

"OK, I have got you this money," he said,. "So now, for God's sake pay those bloody engineers and tell them to get at least one aircraft ready to take me to Malaysia within days. I am not well and do not want the public to know this."

"As you wish, Comrade President," intoned the ageing Minister of Finance. Ageing because his job was one long juggling act trying to keep all but the most essential creditors at bay with an ever decreasing income. This last demand was hardly essential but a request that he could not refuse if he wanted to keep his job, despite the long relationship with his president, dating back to the days of the liberation struggle.

Reluctantly he transferred all the money to the account of the national airline with instructions that all engineers should be paid all their wages in full plus all back pay. Within days one of the ageing, long-haul Boeing 737s was airworthy again and, despite desperate pleas from the chairman of that airline to allow him to sell seats on flights to London and so obtain some income, the aircraft was bound for Kuala Lumpa. It took the President, his wife, two children, ten personal body-guards and some twenty other hangers-on, who had to be kept 'onside', to Kuala Lumpa where it remained for two days before flying the whole party back home again. By this time a few more problems had manifested themselves on the elderly craft and it was again deemed un-airworthy and grounded.

The engineers, however, were delighted; they had not been paid anything for months and had only gone on strike as an absolute last resort. All had run up enormous amounts of credit, mainly with their local supermarkets, who reckoned that they were reasonable risks and likely to get paid at some stage. So it was to these supermarkets that a host of engineers made an early call and paid off the debts that they had accumulated over all those months. Needless to say the supermarkets were also delighted as the amount totalled about $ 2,000,000.

They were particularly glad to receive this large influx of cash as they themselves had huge outstanding accounts with milling companies who had been supplying them with maize meal and flour – two staple foodstuffs for the indigenous community.

So the milling companies also were delighted to receive about $2,000,000 as they owed all of this to the farmers who had supplied them with the maize and wheat which they had turned into mealie meal and flour.

The farmers had been demanding payment for many months now as they badly needed these funds to finance the current year's crop. They had already bought their fertiliser on credit from the fertiliser companies. These companies would not extend any further credit as they owed some $2,000,000 to the government in Value Added Tax [VAT] and already nasty little men in dark glasses had been visiting their warehouses and seeking the manager.

It was therefore a great relief to be able to send some $2,200,000 to the Ministry of Finance in payment of this VAT.

It was nine o' clock on the morning of the 30th day since the $2,000,000 had been received from the bank in EG that this sum was paid. The Minister of Finance even dared to ring the president at this early hour and advise him that these funds had been received and what should he do with them?

"Gideon," barked the president down the private line, "I have told you many times not to telephone me at this time – I am exercising. However, in the light of what you tell me I will overlook this liberty and instruct you to transfer the full amount to the account that I gave you in East Guinnea. Attach a personal memo to the president of that country saying, "Thank you for the loan, Comrade, as promised herewith full and final payment plus interest. My health has shown a remarkable upward turn and at least one of our air-craft is up and running. From your grateful friend, RM. PS. Can you let us have another two million litres of diesel as soon as possible, and please tear up that personal cheque that I gave you."

Is this how African finance works? The money was borrowed, five different companies were able to pay their overdue debts and remain in business, yet the loaned money could be repaid in full. Who was the loser? Or winner?

6
Bad Luck

The coup had gone really well and the new Patriotic People's Party [the PPP] had finally toppled the incumbent government who had run the country for the past 30 years. 'Run the country into the ground', was an expression much used by the hierarchy of the PPP. But now they were history. John Godobo, the 'Great' John Godobo, was the new president. Or would be once he was officially sworn in, which was just as soon as a suitable date could be agreed upon for this momentous occasion.

Meanwhile there was still work to do. The ex-president and one time hero of the people had been shot trying to make a getaway with his immediate cronies in a dash for the border. Many of these cronies had met a similar end – and good riddance to them all. But there were still plenty of others who needed to be caught – preferably alive – because it was they who would know where vast hordes of stolen state funds were hidden. There were ways and means of extracting this information, many of them learned from these very same people who had perfected the art of torture to a fine degree.

John Godobo and his new team would need this money to rebuild a shattered nation and, of course, provide suitable remuneration for himself and a selection of new ministers of state. The ex-president's remaining henchmen must be hiding somewhere in the capital as all roads were closed to any traffic and the airport also closed. Armed militia were even now patrolling all these areas. To ensure that no one tried to slip away from the capital under cover of darkness, John Godobo took the very sensible decision to impose a dusk to dawn curfew. This would mean that nobody was allowed to leave their house after dark. Indeed anyone seen on the streets of the capital after the hour of six o' clock would be shot.

John Godobo was a fairly simple man and despite being the newly nominated people's president did not have any of the trappings of power. Not yet! That would surely come once the hidden state funds were discovered. A president must look like a president and at the moment Godobo did not even have a decent vehicle – it was unthinkable! Meanwhile he had to use the battered old Land Rover that he had been using for the past two years when he had been very much on the run from the past regime.

Presidents were expected to speak to their people though and this could certainly be arranged. One of the first things his 'Government' [he liked to use that word despite it not yet being strictly correct] had done was to commandeer the national radio station and shoot the announcer who was trying to tell the people that the old regime was still in control. martial music was now being played and a canned voice telling everyone to remain calm. So now it was essential that John Godobo [the 'Great' John Godobo] spoke to his [he liked that word as well] people.

To achieve this he first had to find someone who knew how to operate the radio station. Everyone who used to run it had been shot. However, Ishmail Takawera pushed his way into the presence of the Great One and announced that, while in exile from the brutal regime that had now been gloriously defeated, he had once worked for the broadcasting company of a neighbouring state and felt sure that he could operate the fairly basic local set-up. Secretly he thought to himself that if he made a success of this he might have a chance of being made Minister of Communications – or some such exalted title – in the forthcoming government.

John Godobo was delighted when Ishmail told him this. Not the bit about his aspirations to become a Minister of State, but the bit about his [maybe] knowing how to operate the local broadcasting station. Ishmail was despatched forthwith [on foot] to Broadcasting House in the middle of the capital and instructed to do all he could to ensure that the president [elect], the 'Great' John Godobo, would be able to address the nation that very evening. But first he must switch off the god dammed martial music which was getting on everybody's nerves. No one could fathom out who had put it on in the first place – or whose voice kept telling the people to keep calm. It must have been something to do with the last president so must be stopped immediately.

Ishmail Takawera found his way across the ravaged city to Broadcasting House and entered a deserted room which clearly contained the wherewithal to broadcast. There was a large machine in the centre surrounded by microphones and a DVD recorder attached to it with a blinking red light which surely was responsible for the martial music. There were also a few dead bodies lying around which slightly unnerved Ishmail. However, with his ministerial aspirations again raising their head, he plunged bravely at the DVD and silenced it. Quite what the listening masses thought when silence suddenly descended on their living rooms, or mud huts in most cases, is not known. They would be glad that the martial music had finally stopped but probably worried that there might have been a counter-coup. Ishmail was no fool and realised this. So grasping what he hoped was the correct microphone, he pressed a switch leading to it, cleared his throat loudly and, in what he dearly hoped was a ministerial voice, said, "People of this great land, in a few moments your new president will address the nation soon. He will be addressing the nation very soon. Do not switch off your radios as the new president will soon address the nation." He paused, then added, "Very soon."

Not quite knowing what to do next he put the martial music back on. But he was well pleased with himself and hurried back across town to tell the president [elect] – he realised that he had omitted the 'elect' bit in his announcement but did not think it really mattered, that all was ready for the presidential address to the nation.

The 'Great' John Godobo then walked to his battered Land Rover and drove himself to Broadcasting House. Naturally he took a few aides with him, as befits a president [elect] as well as Ishmail, of course. They entered the upstairs room, averted their eyes from the corpses, and advanced on the microphone which Ishmail assured them was The One.

"Shall I introduce you, Your Excellency?" asked Ishmail nervously and, for just a fleeting moment, toyed with the idea of starting the broadcast by saying that it was the Minister of Communications [elect] speaking.

"Please do so," said John Godobo in a deep resonating voice which he dearly hoped sounded presidential.

Ishmail switched off the martial music, [relief throughout the kingdom!], cleared his throat loudly and intoned, "People of our beloved country, I told you that our new president would speak to you very soon and now I have the honour of presenting to you The Honourable, the 'Great' John Godobo." He was not certain if it was in order to tag on 'The Honourable' bit but it sounded good and John Godobo seemed to approve so he hastily added, "Here he is," and pressed the microphone into the Great One's outstretched hand.

John Godobo also cleared his throat – he had never spoken on the radio before and was not entirely sure how to start. He had never been a president [elect] before either for that matter. A deep voice was essential, so with great deliberation he rasped, "Great people of our great land this is your president, the 'Great' John Godobo speaking." He reckoned that having called them great he could use the same adjective for himself and there was really no point in adding the 'elect' bit. "I address you on this momentous day with pride and humility, the wicked old regime has finally been defeated and it is my privilege to lead you, my people, to a new era of prosperity, freedom, reform and happiness in a land risen from the depth of Stygian hell and despair to one of sunlit uplands and hope." He was not too sure what Stygian meant but no one else would either and it sounded good. "However," he continued, "there are still elements of the vicious, crooked old regime at large in our capital city. These enemies of the people – your enemies – are hiding here and will be trying to escape from the city and run for the border. We must catch them and bring them to justice." No point in mentioning the bit about their knowledge of stolen state funds. "To this end my security forces – YOUR security forces – are searching diligently at this very minute. There are armed patrols on the streets and gunmen posted in crucial areas throughout the city. So as to protect you, my people, I am forced to impose a curfew. No one will be allowed out of their house after the hour of 6pm or before 6am. If you are seen on the streets during these hours of darkness you might be shot. This is only for a short time until we can find the traitors lurking amongst us."

There was more to follow with many promises of happiness and great wealth under his great leadership, but finally he ran out of breath and concluded this, his first address to the nation, with the words, "So my beloved people the future is bright and we will march on together in freedom and peace – but please do not go out on the streets after dark until I tell you. Farewell for now from your new president, the 'Great' John Godobo."

After this stirring speech he was emotionally drained and handed the microphone back to Ishmail. They would have liked to have played the National Anthem but could not find a recording of it so, for lack of anything else, put the martial music back on.

It was getting late now and the 'Great' John Godobo wanted to get back to his base as there was still much work to do. He stepped out of Broadcasting House and was shot dead by a gunman patrolling the street on the president [elect's] orders. What bad luck!

7
Banks

Jim was a good farmer. He had been brought up on his father's tobacco farm in Rhodesia, had been to agricultural college in Australia and worked as an under manager for one of the best farmers back in his home country. But now he had his own farm and wanted to make a real success of it. But having put a down payment on the place he had no money left to develop it. This was not an unusual situation for a young man starting out on his own and, with the security of the farm itself as well as his excellent qualifications, any decent bank should be prepared to lend sufficient money for him to get started.

So Jim, armed with his agricultural degree and a good reference letter from his previous employer, made an appointment to see Mr Gomes at the local branch of the Standard Bank. Rhodesia in the early 1960s was only too keen to encourage young, well-qualified men to expand the prosperous tobacco industry and Jim entered Mr Gomes' office with some confidence.

Mr Gomes was also quite young and the post of manager in the town's local branch was his first. He was a small, pale man but neatly dressed and had a cushion on the chair as he sat behind a large impressive desk. Jim was a large man, deeply tanned by the African sun and dressed in the khaki shorts and desert boots, known locally as 'vellies', with no socks which was pretty much the traditional dress of a Rhodesian farmer in those days. Mr Gomes was not a country man so his appointment to this rural branch of the bank was perhaps not the best idea. He felt inferior to Jim and took an immediate and unjustified dislike to him.

"Please sit down, Mr Baker," he said quickly, as Jim towered over him. Jim had a large envelope in his hand which contained all the documents that he thought the bank manager would want to see. He placed this on the desk as he sat down on the chair indicated opposite Mr Gomes.

Ostentatiously, Gomes pushed the envelope back towards Jim and said, "I'll ask to see whatever is in that when I am ready to have a look, if I feel it necessary."

"Sorry," said Jim, retrieving the envelope and putting it on his knees, "the envelope contains my university diploma and letters of reference which I thought you would want to see."

"Yes, yes, maybe. Now, how old are you, Mr. Baker?"

"Twenty-seven."

"Twenty-seven! And you want to borrow seventy-five thousand pounds to grow a crop that you have never grown before, on land you have never cultivated before with labour who have never worked for you before." It was a statement not a question.

"Well, I have grown tobacco before, my farm is in the same area as the one I worked on for three years and I have brought some of the guys who worked for me there with me."

"Oh! Stealing labour from your old employer – is that a decent thing to do?"

"It was done with the complete agreement of my boss, Bill Haskins, and the labour concerned."

"Alright, alright, but working on your own, using your own money – or rather my money," Gomes grinned mirthlessly," is a vast difference from doing it all for an experienced old farmer."

Jim, by nature, was a very even tempered, friendly sort of young man but this obviously aggressive attitude from someone who he had been led to believe would be only too glad to help him, was upsetting him a lot.

"I know of no other way to get started and contemporaries of mine – with less experience, I might add – have successfully borrowed similar sums of money from their banks. I was advised that the Standard Bank also lent money in similar circumstances. Am I wrong?"

Now Mr. Gomes knew that it was his job to lend money to farmers and generate business for the bank but he saw no reason why he should not make this great hunk of a man grovel to him a bit. So he lent back in his chair, fiddled with a pen and said slowly,

"Mr Baker, please do not presume to teach me my job. Certainly my bank is prepared to finance certain individuals whom they consider safe investments. Farmers who we can be certain will repay loans as per our agreement."

"It is certainly my intention to honour any agreement, but farming in Africa – or anywhere for that matter – can have unexpected problems," said Jim, trying very hard to control his temper.

"Exactly!" retorted Gomes. "Seventy-five thousand pounds is a lot of money to invest in a youngster who lacks the experience to cope with these problems."

"So am I wasting my time – and yours?"

"I sincerely hope not. My bank might consider lending you some of the money you require to embark on this adventure given sufficient guarantees. For a start fill in this application form and attach it to those letters, or whatever they are, that you have in that envelope. We will also require someone, not a relation, who knows you well and can back you as a guarantor in case you default on your obligations." Gomes was on firmer ground now and knew exactly what he could insist on.

"You mean I have to ask a friend to pay my debts for me if, for whatever reason, I fail to repay a loan on time." Jim was horrified and hated the idea of asking anyone to put their own money on the line for him. He had certainly never heard of this sort of thing before.

"Exactly!" said Gomes. "It is the very least security we will require." So saying, he handed over a large set of forms, several pages long and stood up, indicating that the interview was at an end.

Jim took the forms and left the office in a bit of a daze. He wandered out into the sunlit, dusty street and headed for his pickup truck to be greeted by a cacophony of barking and flurry of tail wagging as his motley selection of dogs in the back saw him approaching. Who on earth could he ask to sponsor him, he wondered – for that is what it amounted to. He drove home and accepted some slices of cold meat and an avocado from his Shona cook boy for lunch and then spent the afternoon wrestling with the lengthy forms.

Filling in forms did not come easily to Jim but by late afternoon he had sort of broken the back of them so picked up his gun, summoned the hysterically excited dogs and went off round his farm to try and shoot a guinea-fowl or francolin for supper.

The following weekend he went to the local sports club, played a few sets of tennis then quenched his thirst at the bar with a few 'cold ones'. A lot of the local farming community were at the club as later on a film was to be shown on the club's ancient projector – 'Mogambo', no less, a film about safaris in Africa and much anticipated by this hunting orientated crowd. Amongst those present was Jim's old boss, Bill Haskins, so with the 'Dutch courage' brought about by three beers, Jim approached him.

"Evening, Mr. Haskins," he said, never considering calling him Bill, "I was just wondering if you could help me a bit – I've just been to the bank about a loan to grow a crop this year and they asked an awful lot of awkward questions and wanted all sorts of guarantees-----Jim stuttered to a stop.

"Wanted you to get someone to sponsor you-stand as guarantor – I'll be bound," said Haskins, laughing. "Did that for my last two managers and haven't had my fingers burned yet so see no reason for not doing it for you. Where's their goddam form – how I hate the wretched things. You don't deal with that little creep, Gomes, at the Standard, do you?"

"Well, yes, I do and he was pretty demanding and asked a lot of questions."

"Jumped up little twerp trying to establish his authority – he'll lend you the money alright, it's the bank's policy, but he will demand all sorts of security. Here, give me their form and I'll sign it straight away." A quick scribble with the pen that Jim produced and Haskins handed it back adding, "there you are. What are you drinking? Castle? Film's about to start."

A few days later Jim returned to the bank having made the required appointment for ten o'clock. He was kept waiting until ten-thirty but tried not to show his impatience. Gomes was behind his desk as usual shuffling papers in an ostentatious way and did not look up as Jim sat down. Still not looking up, he suddenly stretched his hand out clicking his fingers as he did so. Assuming Gomes did not want him to shake the thin, pale projection offered, he guessed correctly and placed the sheaf of papers he was carrying into it.

Gomes still did not look up but after a few minutes started thumbing through the copious forms. Every now and again he made a note on a pad in front of him and finally did look up and appeared surprised to see Jim sitting there.

"Ah! Mr Baker," he said, "so these are your application forms for the required loan – you really should have completed them in black ink but we will overlook that for the moment. I see that you are applying for this loan in the name of a company – Best Smoke Investments [Pvt Ltd] – with yourself as the managing director and one Fiona Watkins as the only other director. Who, pray, is Miss / Mrs Fiona Watkins?"

"Fiona Watkins is a highly qualified accountant who does my books for me and will be responsible for my year end tax returns, balance sheet etc. I sincerely hope that in the not too distant future she will also become my wife."

"Ah! How nice," said Gomes, who was unmarried himself. "All quite cosy. Nevertheless, before we can consider risking this considerable sum on your farming venture I must insist on your lodging with me the following:

1] A notarial covering bond on your farm.
2] A similar bond on all your moveable assets such as tractors, farm implements etc.
3] A stop order with the Rhodesia Tobacco Association for £79,500 which represents the capital and interest on this loan and will be paid to me – er, this bank – in full before anything is paid to you.
4] You must take out a life insurance policy with ourselves as the sole beneficiary so that in the event of your demise before the loan is fully repaid we are safeguarded.

5] A personal guarantee from yourself that this loan will be repaid in full and on time despite any misfortune befalling Best Smoke Investments [Pvt Ltd].

6] A guarantee from your sponsor that he will repay this loan should you or your company default.

7] A similar guarantee from the other director – Miss Watkins.

Is that all clear?"

"Nothing else?" said a numb and shocked Jim with a small, wry grin.

Jim did eventually get his loan having mortgaged himself absolutely up to the hilt and got the required guarantees. By the end of his first tobacco season he was able to repay it all with just a little extra, but enough to persuade Fiona to marry him and to go on a short honeymoon. But with a new season looming he was forced to revisit the bank and talk again to Mr Gomes who was still the local manager. Gomes had not been invited to the wedding which had been attended by most of the local farmers and even a few of the town's businessmen.

Much the same procedure was re-enacted with Jim finally emerging with a seasonal loan very similar to his first one. Again, by the end of that season he was able to repay it all but the small extra was soon used up by his having to buy the vast amount of equipment required for a newborn baby boy. Over the next few years the same sort of pattern continued – there were two more children and school fees began to rear their head. Then came UDI when Ian Smith, the Prime Minister, unilaterally declared that, henceforth, Rhodesia was an independent country. Sanctions were implemented and tobacco sales slumped. Jim was forced to diversify into other crops like wheat, fruit and coffee. More money was needed to develop these crops and there were many painful visits to the bank.

Gomes had moved on by now and a selection of new managers came and went; some were sympathetic and helpful, others surly and unhelpful, but Jim and his family somehow survived. Then the 'Bush War' started with incursions of terrorists from across the border in Zambia. As a fit young man

Jim was soon called up and joined the local PATU stick – a team of four or five to act as a Police Anti-Terrorist Unit. This meant frequent absences from his isolated farm while Fiona and the three children went to stay with her mother in town.

Inevitably the farm suffered and at the end of the 1974 season Jim was unable to repay his loan in full.

With the end of the war and Independence Jim was once again able to concentrate on his farming. Money was more freely available and with the new coffee and fruit crops now well established, there was a very handy supplement to be added to the annual income from the main crop which was still tobacco. Slowly Jim discovered that year by year he had to borrow less and less from the bank each year until – Bingo! In the late 1980s he had no need to borrow anything to grow the next year's crop. Three years later he was voted Tobacco Grower of the Year by his peers and he was making so much money that he wondered what to do with the surplus.

There was yet another new bank manager at the Standard and Jim went to see him. He was quite young like Gomes had been, quite arrogant as well but had to treat Jim with considerable respect as he was now very much one of the area's leading farmers and a pillar of the community.

"I have far too much money in my current account, Mr Harris," Jim began after being told to sit down and offered a cup of coffee, "I have bought all the fertiliser and crop chemicals that I will need for the coming season and I don't want a lot of cash sitting in my account earning no income – any suggestions?"

"Well, yes," said Harris, "we as a bank can offer you very attractive investment terms if you leave your money with us on a fixed deposit over a reasonable length of time."

"OK" said Jim, with a smile, "I will leave my money invested in your bank, but I will need a few guarantees."

"Yes, of course. We will offer you our usual sliding scale of interest depending on how long you leave the funds with us and how much."

"Guarantees that my money will be safe are what I mean."

Harris laughed easily. "You are dealing with a bank, Mr Baker, not some tinpot little company newly listed on the local stock exchange."

"Exactly! Your bank wanted security from me and if I leave my hard-earned money here I want security from you." Jim drew a piece of paper from his elephant skin briefcase.

"Mr Harris, before I let your bank have my money for investment purposes I shall require the following:

1]   A notarial covering bond on this building.
2]   A similar bond on all moveable assets such as desks, tables, computers etc.
3]   A stop order on any sales that the bank makes.
4]   You must take out a life insurance policy with me as the beneficiary in case you die while my money is with this bank and I am unhappy with your successor.
5]   A personal guarantee from yourself that you will refund me all my money plus any interest due should this bank go under.
6]   A guarantee from some sort of sponsor that should this bank and yourself fail to repay me my money in full that they will. A fellow bank perhaps?
7]   A similar guarantee from one of your directors.

I don't think I am asking too much. It's what you wanted from me."

10
Niece

Flying immediately after the Second World War was a much more special occasion than it is today. It is commonplace these days – everyone flies and thinks nothing of it. In the late 1940s it was a big deal. You changed into respectable clothes, took out 'flight insurance' and sent telegrams back home to confirm your safe arrival. Now-a-days it is just like catching a bus – except for the ever-increasing security checks, of course.

In 1950 my 16-year-old niece had never flown so it was with great excitement and some trepidation that in the summer holidays she was booked to fly from London to Paris to visit me, her uncle and godfather. I was living near the Sorbonne at that time studying renaissance art – particularly that of the 16th century. My niece, Amelia, was my sister's eldest child and a very pretty one too although at that stage of her life totally naïve. The idea was that a couple of weeks in Paris away from immediate family would broaden her outlook on life and do her a world of good. I was very fond of her and more than happy to have her to stay with my wife and me in our rented apartment.

She was put on a British European Airways plane by her mother and given all sorts of advice about how to behave, not to speak to strangers, be polite to my wife and generally look after her appearance. Having been issued with a boarding pass she bid her parents good-bye and passed through immigration and customs into the departure lounge. Here she sat demurely on a seat, looked at the boarding pass and saw she had been allocated seat number 18F. Where would that be, she wondered and who would be in 18E or G. This was a worry and she looked round at her fellow passengers trying to decide who she would like it to be. This was not very encouraging. Most were smartly dressed, serious looking businessmen carrying briefcases.

The flight was called and Amelia joined the well-mannered passengers in the queue who presented their boarding cards to a hostess and was shown her seat. It turned out to be a window seat with just one other next to it bordering the aisle. This was still unoccupied as, with some suppressed excitement, she eased her way into the seat and experimented with how to fasten the seat belt. However, it was not long before an elderly gentleman smiled at her and started removing a light coat prior to taking the vacant seat. Amelia glanced at him but wary of what her mother had said about strange men, did not return the smile. In that brief glance though she had noticed one thing. Having removed his coat she could now see that he was wearing a clerical collar – or 'dog collar', as her father called it. Somehow this reassured her and she felt she could have done a lot worse by way of seat companions.

Then came the excitement of take-off. Having progressed slowly to the end of the runway the 'plane came thundering back down it and amazingly started lifting into the air. Amelia gripped the armrest of her seat and only just prevented herself from squealing with excitement. Up and up went the plane and Amelia's ears started to pop. Soon the captain told passengers that they could undo their seat belts and drinks were served. A smiling air hostess gave Amelia an orange squash but while trying to lower the little table in front of her she spilt some of this on her fingers and dress. This embarrassed her a lot and fumbling for her handkerchief she spilt a lot more. The clergyman on the next seat looked at her and frowned – no smile this time.

She was now very flustered but remembered being told that aeroplanes these days had lavatories so she decided to make use of this facility and tidy herself up. This, of course, meant getting past the clergyman to reach the aisle and walk to the lavatory located near the tail of the plane.

With poor grace he shifted himself sideways and she slid past but in doing so dropped her handkerchief. She did not dare stop and try to retrieve it but just bolted for the safety of the loo. Here she did sponge off most of the spilt orange juice and, taking a deep breath, braced herself to getting past the clergyman again. This time he did actually get up to let her pass but in doing so she kicked him quite hard on the shins and stumbled in an untidy heap onto her seat. He said nothing in reply to her muttered 'sorry' but his mouth was set in a hard, straight line.

For nearly half an hour after this she just sat very still and looked out of the window. Then she remembered the dropped handkerchief. Where was it? Cautiously she looked around. Not on the floor at her feet. Nor was she sitting on it. She glanced across at her grumpy neighbour and was surprised to see that he had drifted off to sleep, letting the newspaper he was reading fall onto his chest – and there, just peeping out from below the bottom of the newspaper, was the white linen corner of her handkerchief lying on his lap.

Right, she thought, this is my chance. He is asleep and if I make a quick grab for the handkerchief and whisk it away he is unlikely even to wake up and I will not have the embarrassment of asking him if I can have it back.

Very slowly she moved her left hand across and grasped the corner of the handkerchief between her finger and thumb. With a quick flick she pulled it towards her.

Unfortunately, it was not the handkerchief. It was the corner of the clergyman's shirt just peeping out between an undone fly button. I leave it to your imagination as to what the result of a sharp pull on this garment would be.

11
News Time

Just after the First World War, an enterprising young editor started a farming magazine in Kenya to try and cater for the ever increasing, but widespread, farming community that was scattered far and wide across the colony.

He enlisted the help of experts to write articles about cattle diseases, pest control in crops, how to effectively clear your land of thorn scrub and a multitude of other pressing issues important to the new farmers. He got merchants in Nairobi to advertise their goods and where to buy much needed things like cattle dip, fencing wire, fertiliser, tractors and other farm implements. He even persuaded hotels and restaurants to tell farmers where to go for a night's rest or good meal when they came to town.

He did a very good job and in no time his little weekly magazine was much appreciated by the farming community. But the main problem was how to get it to the people who really wanted to read it. The postal service was very erratic at best and non-existent for some of the more isolated farms. The best way of getting post for any farm remotely near rail was to have a bag kept at the nearest station, have their post put in this and held by the stationmaster until such time as the farmer could collect it. Some, who lived relatively close to a station, would send a youth on foot to collect the precious bag every day. This would often entail a 15-mile hike in each direction – no wonder Kenya today produces such fine long-distance runners!

The keen young editor's magazine was reaching a lot of farmers, but after an initial rush of subscribers, orders tailed off badly and some were even cancelled because the magazine was largely out of date when received at some of the more remote farms.

Being keen and young the editor, who was very proud of his little magazine, decided to go himself to some of these remote communities, speak to the farmers on the ground and see what could be done to ensure that they were able to get his magazine in reasonable time. He met a very diverse selection of characters, but most said that they found the magazine very useful and relied heavily on it for much needed information concerning their farming activities, as well as appreciating up to date news on where to stay and what was going on in the social circles of Nairobi. Apart from the train method, some got their post delivered by bus, while others collected it from a local store, which was usually run by an old Indian trader.

Towards the end of his visit to one remote area, the editor went to see an old man who lived on his own in the 'back of beyond'. After receiving a welcome cup of tea he sat with the old man on his veranda overlooking a beautiful sweep of grassland on which a considerable amount of wild game was peacefully grazing. Their conversation went something like this:

"What a wonderful view you've got, it must be very peaceful living here," enthused the editor.

"It's peaceful enough, but getting any sort of supplies is a real problem, let alone your magazine," responded the old settler.

"Where do you get your supplies?"

"From old Joti Ram who runs that grotty little store about twenty miles back towards the village."

"Is that where you pick up my magazine?"

"Sure do, but even that is not always there."

"What do you do then?"

"Well, if the magazine isn't there, I just have to use grass!"

12
My New Friend

"So you actually did nothing to prevent this vicious dog from attacking a sister who you have told the court that 'you did not get on with particularly well'".

It was a very unkind and difficult question for me to answer so perhaps I had better give you the background to what happened.

My late husband had never liked dogs. It was something that I never really understood as he was a gentle man and very tolerant of most things. But he was also meticulously tidy and I suspect that it was because dogs could be a bit unpredictable and consequently untidy that he objected to them being in his home. As a result, in all our very happy forty-five years of marriage, we never owned a dog – or cat for that matter. I had grown up with several dogs always around my parents' home and at first missed having one terribly.

So it was that when my dear husband eventually succumbed to cancer after a long and painful illness I decided to have a dog again. Nothing could replace my beloved Tom, of course, and the children were very good at calling in to see me and I loved getting to know the grandchildren, but they had their own lives to be getting on with and I found our little cottage an empty and sad place after the initial turmoil following the funeral.

I rang up my sister and told her what I was thinking of doing. I knew that she had always had dogs and would possibly know how I could get one as I was woefully ignorant about how to go about it. I have to tell you straight away that for some years I had not been getting on particularly well with Judith, my younger sister. Her husband, Giles Parsons, had done extremely well in the City – banking, hedge funds, asset management or something that I never understood. As a result they had bought a large house in nearby Gloucestershire and moved out of our society and income bracket. Although still not far away from us we had never been invited to visit. I regret to say that I suspected her of being rather contemptuous about Tom's, not very well paid job, as an accountant in our small town. This saddened me a lot as Tom always did a sound, honest day's work and, while we did not have many expensive holidays, there was always adequate food on the table and our three children all had perfectly good educations.

So it was with a slight feeling of nervousness that I dialled her number. It was immediately apparent that she was in a bit of a state.

"Oh! It's you is it Rose?" she said," Yes, what do you want? I have problems of my own here at the moment."

I nearly said that I would ring back later as I selfishly did not want to get involved with her problems. But having taken the plunge of ringing her I was determined to seek her advice. But I did preface my request by asking what the problem was.

"You would not understand," she almost snapped at me, "that lovely, sweet little terrier that Giles gave me for my last birthday is lost and I am at my wits end trying to find her. We went for a walk yesterday evening and she chased a rabbit into the wood and I have not seen her since. I have tried – but you would not understand never having owned a dog."

"Oh! But I do understand," I hastened to say, "I know how much you love your dogs and it must be very worrying to have lost yours – where could it have gone?"

"If I could answer that question she would not be lost," Judith replied, rather unkindly. But then relented, by adding, "I expect she will turn up eventually as she has gone missing for short periods before when chasing rabbits. Anyway, what did you ring up about?"

"Actually it was about dogs," I answered rather hesitantly. "As you know Tom and I never had one but now that he is gone, the house seems so quiet and empty that I thought a little dog might be a welcome companion in my old age. I was ringing you to ask if you knew how I set about getting one."

There was a brief silence at the other end of the line, then "Rose, have you any idea what owning a dog involves? It is alright for us with a large house and garden but in your pokey little cottage and no real garden it will be underfoot all the time and a constant source of worry. I strongly advise you against such an idea. A cat is a possibility. Cats are much more independent and quite clean – yes, think about a cat but definitely not a dog."

We did not talk much more after that and I put the receiver down feeling very deflated and depressed. I wanted a dog, not a cat.

Then I had a good idea. I would go and speak to our local vet. We had never had occasion to use his services but he had been at school with Tom years ago and we had remained friends after he and his wife moved to a practice in the next village. Surely he would know a lot about dogs and how to get one.

Next day I took the bus round to his village and, after asking the receptionist if I could have a brief word with Mr Rogers, I was about to sit down and wait when my eye was attracted to a notice board at the side of the receptionist's desk. There were numerous bits of paper pinned to it advertising things like dog food, kennels at which one could board a dog, forthcoming shows and several other things. But at the bottom there was a small notice advertising "Puppies for Sale". I read it and learned that I could purchase an eight week old Border terrier for £250! Never in my wildest dreams had I thought that a puppy would cost that much – clearly I could not afford anything like that. Then there would be the cost of looking after it. Was my whole idea of getting a dog a mad pipe dream?

My depressing thoughts were interrupted by the receptionist saying that Mr Rogers had a free moment between patients and would be delighted if I would go through to his surgery straight away.

Geoff Rogers had been at Tom's funeral and had actually been one of the pall-bearers to carry the coffin on its last sad journey. So he greeted me warmly and put a comforting arm round my shoulder accompanied by a peck on the cheek. He had always been a nice man and, as he was much the same age as Tom would have been, must be due to retire quite soon.

"Well, well, Rose dear. What brings you to my humble surgery?" he smiled at me.

"I want your help or advice, Geoff," I said, smiling back at him. "I have decided that I would like a small dog to keep me company in my old age now that Tom has gone. Do you think it is a good idea? And if so, how do I go about getting one?" Then, before he could reply, I added hastily, "But judging by the price of puppies as advertised in your reception I really doubt very much if I could afford it."

Geoff smoked a pipe [not something I really approved of but better than cigarettes]. Now he took it out of his pocket and started going through the elaborate routine of packing the bowl with tobacco and tamping it down before replying. All the while he was looking at me and not at what he was doing with the pipe. Eventually he said, "Rose, you have never to my knowledge owned a dog so cannot realise what a huge responsibility and commitment it is. And expensive – you are right." He paused and struck a match, put the pipe in his mouth and lit it. I have to admit that I rather liked the rich tobacco smell that wafted across the room. Geoff waved the smoke away from in front of his face and continued, "But I am a lover of dogs. They are the most wonderful companions in this world. Not for nothing are they called 'Man's Best Friend'. The right dog would bring you enormous happiness and love in your latter years."

This was cheering news and I smiled at him again but said nothing as he was obviously going to continue. His pipe had gone out by now but he waved it about as he spoke.

"If you really do want a dog, Rose, I will certainly be of all the help I can. Tom was a very good friend of mine – as you are – and it would give me a lot of pleasure to help, in some small way, to ease the grief of Tom's departure. However, you must be careful. I do not recommend that you take on a puppy. They are very sweet, very cheeky, very demanding and make messes everywhere as well as tearing up anything left lying around – and expensive! No, you do not want a puppy. There are many excellent dog rescue homes and organisations from which you can often get an older dog but there is a risk here, as you would have no knowledge as to what sort of problems the dog had in the past or why it had been abandoned or strayed. You could be letting yourself in for a lot of trouble."

My mood dropped again. Geoff now seemed to be cancelling out all the optimistic words he had used to encourage me before. My face obviously betrayed my feelings because he went on quickly,

"In my little practice here I am quite often told about dogs that are in need of a new home. Sometimes the owner dies – we are very much a retired community around here, you know. Sometimes a dog is lost and the police would much rather I try to find the owner than them. They claim that I have the facilities to look after the dog better than they, so I do usually oblige and can often locate the owner. Then there are dogs given to children for Christmas and after the initial excitement it becomes patently obvious that the household is totally unsuitable for a dog. When the children go back to school and the parents both go to work the dog is just left to fend for itself. We work very closely with the RSPCA and do on occasion remove dogs from such situations. So, what I will do is to keep my eye out for the sort of dog that I think might suit you and, if it is obvious that a new owner is required for whatever reason, I will give you a ring and get you to come and have a look."

This sounded marvellous but one immediate question sprang to mind. "What might it cost?" I blurted out.

"Rose, I am a vet – and a friend – I do not make money out of finding nice homes for dogs. There just could be a few minor expenses if the dog is injured in any way and requires my professional services. But you will have to be patient as I cannot guarantee anything and it could be some time before we get what I consider is a suitable dog for you."

With that, I thanked Geoff very much, watched him hastily put away his pipe as a young man entered carrying a very sick looking parrot, and left the surgery.

It sounded like very sound advice from someone who was not only a good friend but very knowledgeable about dogs as well. I settled down back in my comfortable little cottage ['pokey' was a very unkind word I thought], and would try to be patient waiting for word from Geoff.

Imagine my surprise then when under a fortnight later [12 days actually] the telephone rang and, in a quiet voice, Geoff asked if I could come round and see him that very afternoon.

"Have you found me a dog?" I could not resist asking.

"Well, maybe. Just pop round and we'll see."

I was at the bus stop sharp at two o'clock and in Geoff's surgery just before 2.45pm. The receptionist smiled at me and said I would have to wait a few minutes as the man with the parrot was back in with Mr Rogers and 'it was not looking too good'.

It is hard to tell if a parrot is looking better or not, but shortly the man emerged from Geoff's room holding the wretched bird tenderly as Geoff patted his arm and assured him that it now 'had a very good chance of complete recovery'. "Ah! Rose," he added as he saw me, "Come in."

Beside his desk, in a small wire cage was a very bedraggled, thin, sad looking, little brown and white terrier. As I neared the desk it looked up at me, the little ears cocked up, head went on one side and a stumpy tail wagged just twice. My heart lurched. I had never seen anything so sweet and pathetic and in need of so much love.

Without taking my eyes off the little dog, I whispered to Geoff, "Is that it?"

I suppose he said, 'yes' but I really don't know because by now I was on my knees fumbling with the fastening of the cage. I just wanted to take the little animal in my arms and cuddle it.

"Hey! Steady on, old girl," I did hear Geoff chuckle. Then he was on his knees beside me, lifting the little dog out of the cage and handing her to me. It was a little girl, or bitch as they are called in doggy language [I don't really like that word though]. I held her tight and she pressed a little wet nose against my cheek and a very small pink tongue shot out from between a set of lovely, sharp little teeth and gave me a couple of quick licks. She then nestled down against my bosom, gave a little wriggle and a grunt before closing her eyes and, as far as I could tell, falling asleep.

Geoff had said nothing more all this time but now he stood up with a broad grin all over his face. "I have never really believed in 'love at first sight'," he said, "but I do believe that I have just seen proof of it."

The rest of that afternoon passed in a bit of a blur and it was not until I caught the last bus home and arrived at the cottage with my little treasure back in her cage and an armful of bits and pieces that were deemed necessary for her continued comfort, that I had time to recall all I had been told.

The little dog had been brought in to Geoff's surgery some ten days previously. She was covered in mud, obviously starving and totally exhausted. She wore no collar or any other form of identification and Geoff had feared for her life. But a warm bath to remove all the mud, a good meal and a couple of injections had revived her and now, another week later, she was out of all danger and well on the way to complete recovery.

Geoff had notified the police, the RSPCA, a couple of dog rescue homes and put up notices in all nearby villages in an attempt to find the owner of the little dog but, as no one had come forward, he had decided that it was quite fair to try and find a new owner. And that is where I came in.

I named the little girl, Jessy, and she very quickly recognised it as her name. I bought her a cosy little basket which I kept in the kitchen and she lay in this watching me cook. We went for lovely little walks in the nearby fields but I kept her on a lead as the naughty little thing wanted to chase any bunny rabbit or even bird that we saw. At night I regret to say she slept on my bed – and very cosy we were too. We were very happy.

That could have been the end of the story but a month or so later I rang up my sister Judith again to tell her how very happy I was now that I had this lovely little companion.

"Good Heavens!" she said, "you don't mean to say you actually got a dog – despite my advice – I never found mine, you know."

Then, rather against my better judgement, I invited Judith round to come and see Jessy. Somewhat to my surprise she agreed to come and, as she had not been to my home for some two years I baked a cake and bought some Earl Grey tea instead of the 'builders' tea that I drink. I gave Jessy a bath – which she does not really like – and waited for my sister's arrival.

Shortly after four o' clock a large BMW car drew up outside the cottage and Judith got out and walked towards me. I walked out to meet her with Jessy trotting along at my heels. As I stopped, Jessy continued walking and suddenly came face to face with Judith. She halted and stood for a moment stock still, then slowly the hair on her back started to rise and a sinister little growl rumbled in her throat. Judith stopped also and looked down at my dog; she started to say something but at the sound of her voice Jessy leapt at her and fastened her teeth into Judith's throat. I was terrified; Judith was tearing at the dog with her hands and screaming while Jessy was shaking away at her throat as though it were a rabbit. In her struggles Judith slipped and fell so was soon rolling around on the path to my house with Jessy getting more and more excited and aggressive. It was not long before I saw a stream of blood starting to pump out of Judith's throat and, although she had hold of Jessy and was pulling at her back legs, she seemed to be totally incapable of making the dog let go of the vice-like grip it had on her throat. I can't really remember very clearly exactly what I was doing as this nightmarish scene unfolded before my horrified eyes. I know that I was screaming for help and shouting at Jessy then I did aim a kick at the dog to try and get it to let go of my sister's throat but I am not used to doing this sort of thing and I also overbalanced and fell in an untidy heap on top of the struggling woman and dog. Jessy was uttering excited growls, Judith was still screaming and I found myself suddenly drenched with blood which spurted into my face, temporarily blinding me. I staggered to my feet mopping frantically at my face and stumbled away from the terrifying battle on the path. I did manage to smear some of the blood out of my eyes and looked back at what was happening.

Judith had stopped screaming by now and was just lying quite still with her left leg twitching slightly. Jessy, covered in blood herself, continued to growl and worry at the now lacerated throat of my sister. Never having owned a dog, I had no idea what to do. My dear little pet was acting like a demented wild animal and I was terrified. I ran to the house and dialled 999 before collapsing in a chair. I think I passed out then because the next thing I remember was a policeman standing over me and calling my name. I stood up shakily and looked outside. There were more policemen there looking at a bundle on the ground covered by a white sheet. There was no sign of Jessy.

"That is really all I can tell you, Your Honour."

The prosecuting council then continued to question me further. "I put it to you," he said in that irritating, pompous manner that legal people tend to adopt, "That you knew your dog was a vicious, dangerous monster and that, far from trying to prevent it from attacking a sister you loathed and envied, you actually egged it on and encouraged it to attack her. I agree that it is unlikely that you actually wanted the dog to kill your sister but it was your clear intention that it should cause her grievous bodily harm. Further, Mr Rogers, the veterinary surgeon you mentioned, warned you that the dog he gave you needed very special attention and that he was only letting you have it on condition you kept it on a lead at all times when in public."

He then produced a well-thumbed booklet and asked if it was mine.

I thought I had hidden that thing but could not deny that it was mine.

"It is obvious that this book has been thoroughly scrutinised and that you have learned its teachings well," he continued, "so I urge the jury to pass a verdict of guilty on you for planning to seriously injure an innocent person – to wit your sister, Judith Parsons – by training your dog to attack her."

Well, if you do happen to be given a Pit Bull terrier you might as well learn how to train it to do what it does best!!

13
My Grandfather's Car

My grandfather was an eccentric old baronet from North Yorkshire who believed that the only safe means of transport was the horse [probably spelt by him with a capital H]. However, just before WW1 he was persuaded to buy a car. He hated the thing, particularly because it had to be started with a handle sticking out of the front under the bonnet.

After the war [to which he took his horse] he returned to his estate and recommenced his association with the much loathed car. But help was at hand. A smart, young salesman with slicked back hair and a lot of plausible patter heard about my grandfather's problem and drove all the way up from London to try and sell him one of the new Rolls-Royces [which, of course, did not have to be started with a handle].

My grandfather took an immediate and violent dislike to the young salesman, but was very impressed by the car. Particularly so because he could sit warmly inside it behind the steering wheel, press a button and the engine would purr into life.

The salesman opened the bonnet and pointed out all the marvellous new inventions contained therein, talked about fuel consumption, revolutions per minute, acceleration, and braking power all of which went way over my grandfather's head. Then they went through the interior – comfortable bucket seats, an interior light, an armrest etc. etc. My grandfather continued to be impressed [despite the greasy little salesman]. Then, just as he was about to produce his cheque book, he happened to see, under the back seat, a long metal starting handle. He stiffened and shook – visibly upset.

Rounding on the salesman, he said, "What is that?"

"Well, it's an emergency starting handle," said the salesman defensively.

"I thought you said this car NEVER had to be hand started."

"I assure you, Sir Frederick, it does not. It will ALWAYS start first time with the automatic starter." replied the slightly shaken salesman.

"Then what is this starting handle for?"

"Well, it's just there as a sort of accessory because cars have always had one."

"But presumably I am being charged for it and your company would not put it there unless they thought it might be required."

"I assure you, sir, that it will NEVER be required."

"Well, why the dickens, put it in the car, then?"

"We at Rolls-Royce think of every possible eventuality and pride ourselves in looking after our much valued customers whatever the unforeseen occasion."

"So what you are saying is that this very expensive car COULD have to be hand started. Probably on a very cold morning when it is pouring with rain, I am far from home and my chauffeur is on leave. This was just the problem with my old car and I am not about to write you a huge cheque if this fancy vehicle of yours has exactly the same deficiency." My grandfather was literally about to BURST with indignation.

Despite the cold North Yorkshire air, the salesman was sweating by now and was suddenly conscious that he could yet lose the sale that he had driven all the way up from London to clinch. This old fool had to be won round somehow.

Taking a deep breath [which brought in more cold North Yorkshire air to his lungs and made him cough] he said, "Sir Frederick, would you mind unbuttoning the front of your shirt?"

My grandfather huffed and puffed a bit at this unusual request but eventually did unbutton his thick, cotton shirt and exposed a skinny, hairy chest on which were two, rather cold looking, prominent nipples.

The salesman leaned forward, pointed at these two little protuberances and said, "Sir Frederick, why do you think the Good Lord endowed you with these?"

"I have absolutely no idea, and it has nothing to do with the matter in hand."

"Oh, but it has, the Good Lord endowed you with those little things just IN CASE you have a baby and the likelihood of that happening is about the same as the likelihood of our Rolls-Royce requiring a starting handle. Like the Good Lord we, at Rolls-Royce, think of EVERY eventuality."

My grandfather wrote his cheque!

14
Mistaken Identity

In the days when commercial farming was a thriving concern in Zimbabwe, tobacco was one of the most paying of crops. This was not a particularly easy crop to grow well and needed constant, expert supervision to attain the sort of quality that cigarette makers throughout the world required to put into their lethal product.

Ian Hird was a very good grower and visited his lands frequently every day. Tobacco is a very labour intensive crop and larger farms like Ian's would probably employ three or four hundred workers so the boss would not know all of them personally. Ian would usually drive some of them to where the crop was being grown in a pick-up truck [similar to the Australian Ute] which was a popular choice of vehicle as a multitude of different things, as well as the African workers, could very easily be put in the open back.

Most days Ian would do many trips to the lands loaded down with workers and all the bits and pieces that he might require in the course of a working day, but over a few weeks he became dismayed to realise that all the things that had been in the back of his truck when he set out were not always there on his return. The odd spade, pair of pliers, empty sacks, and a bucket all seemed to have disembarked at the same time as the workers had got off and never re-appeared. This annoyed Ian considerably but he could never work out who was actually removing these items.

One day he set off to the lands with no one in the back of his truck but just the usual selection of odds and ends. He parked the truck by the side of a road and walked into the land to see what progress was being made in the reaping of the tobacco. He was away from his vehicle for about half an hour and as he walked back towards it he saw a youth, just the other side of the road, climbing through the fence with an umbrella.

"The little bastard," he thought to himself. "He's nicked my brolly from the back of the truck." He broke into a run screaming at the youth to stop. Now when an irate farmer shouts at you and starts running towards you, one's automatic reaction is to run away and this is exactly what the youth did.

Ian was young and fit in those days so, despite a start of some 100 metres, he gradually started gaining on the youth. It was not easy though; the grass was long and wet and at least two lines of barbed wire fences had to be negotiated. The youth kept glancing nervously over his shoulder and increasing his pace. Ian was sweating hard by this time and had a deep cut down one arm where he had caught it on the barbed wire fence. He had also lost his hat but was determined to catch the thief. With a desperate spurt over a slightly more even piece of ground he finally managed to come more or less level with his quarry and, with a classic rugby tackle, brought him crashing to the ground. Words were not necessary which was just as well – Ian being very out of breath. They rolled on the wet ground together and Ian, being considerably bigger than the youth, soon managed to snatch the umbrella away from his opponent. Having done so he kicked him firmly up the backside and cuffed him round the ears before turning on his heel and stalking away with his prize firmly grasped in one hand. The terrified youth fled in the opposite direction.

"Not sure who that was," said Ian to himself, "probably one of the workers' sons, but that will teach the little bugger a lesson."

He drove home feeling pretty pleased with himself, stopped in front of the main entrance to the house and walked into the hall wiping his sweaty brow with a handkerchief and mopping at the bleeding arm with another rag. There lying on the hall table was his umbrella!

15
So Near Yet So Far

Zimbabwe is currently very short of fuel and fuel is very important as you cannot go anywhere without it. Long queues of vehicles are a common sight outside any fuel station that just might have some. When a fuel station does get a supply they usually like to ration it out between as many customers as possible so that most people get something.

There is one such supplier quite near us on the outskirts of Harare. Not long ago he got a reasonable supply of fuel and a long queue immediately formed. Taking a look at the queue, the proprietor reckoned that he could sell each motorist just 40 litres of fuel and duly collected $40 from each vehicle after putting in the promised 40 litres. All this took a bit of time, as he had to explain to each driver that he could only have the prescribed amount, and then take the money and often had to find change as well.

Watching all this was Tendai who had recently been employed by the garage but sacked for petty thieving. Petty thieves often have devious, scheming minds and Tendai was no exception. He worked out a cunning plan to make some easy money.

When the next delivery of fuel arrived, he was ready to put his plan into action. One of his successful petty thieving escapades had resulted in his acquiring a rubber stamp bearing the garage's address. Armed with this he put on his old overalls, that still had the name of the garage written on the back, and approached the vehicle at the very back of the queue and therefore out of sight of those on the garage forecourt. He explained to the driver that he would only be allowed to purchase 40 litres of fuel and that it would cost him $ 40 so, to save time, would the driver please give the $40 to him, Tendai, an employee of the garage, in return for which he would receive a stamped receipt which should be presented to the fuel attendant, thus saving a great deal of time.

"Good idea!" thought the driver and happily handed over his $40 getting the receipt from Tendai in exchange.

The next car was equally co-operative and Tendai pocketed another $40. This was too easy he thought and told the next car that the allowance was 60 litres and that he would therefore require $60. A delighted driver happily handed over the cash. Seven cars later and Tendai upped the amount allowed to 80 litres and $80. He did not dare raise the amount any higher but after 25 vehicles he was getting a bit close to the garage anyway and already had $2,000. Then, approaching the last vehicle he intended to 'touch', he hit a snag; the vehicle was a closed van and he was unable to see the driver until he tapped on the window and the man turned round. Tendai was horrified to realise that he knew the guy well, both of them having worked at the garage a few weeks previously. His name was Mishek

"Hello, Tendai," said Mishek. "What do you want?" Then, noticing the garage logo on Tendai's overalls, added, "I thought you had been sacked."

Quick thinking was required. "Sure, I was," admitted Tendai, "but I was allowed to keep my old pair of overalls and I might have landed another job in town, so could you give me a lift if you are going that way?"

"OK," said Mishek, "jump in, but I need a pee so I'll just let the guy behind me go first to get his fuel."

Quick thinking required again! If the guy behind was served before Mishek the cat would be out of the bag.

"Look here, shamwari," he said, "I have just done a deal selling fuel coupons in advance and have about $2,000 here, if you fill up straight away and drive on I'll split it with you – OK?"

Mishek smiled a tight little smile. "That's Tendai for you," he thought, so said, 'let's just see this cash first.''

Tendai quickly handed over the wad of dirty notes.

"Great!" said Mishek, "now get out of my car and beat it before I turn the police onto you."

1 6

Skiing – a warning to beginners

I never had any ambition to ski. The idea of climbing to the top of a mountain in mid-winter just to slide down it again did not appeal to me at all.

However, pressure was brought to bear by my cousin who offered us a share of a chalet in a well-known ski resort and, somewhat ungraciously I agreed to go, reasoning that I could always drink a lot of French wine and perhaps slide down the odd gentle slope on a tea tray to clear my head.

We arrived by air in Geneva and hired a car to follow my cousin to the resort some four hours drive away at a place called Les Arcs, where we were soon comfortably installed overlooking the nursery slopes.

Debate raged as to how we should all handle the approaching ordeal on the morrow. My sons Robert [11] and Harry [9] were told to join Les Enfants Ecole de Ski [even I realised that this meant the children's ski school] and this seemed reasonable so we hired the necessary kit.

I was told that I couldn't have a tea tray, partly because there was not one big enough and partly because it wasn't done anyway. I was told instead that I had to join Les Debutantes. I brightened considerably at this and visualised something young and pretty probably in a white ball gown. I didn't feel that skis would be strictly necessary but, being told that they were, I hired the smallest pair possible which were attached to my feet with the aid of a pair of huge inflexible boots. Pam, my wife, was also joining Les Debutantes and, while I privately thought she was a little too old and might cramp my style, it would have been churlish to say so.

The morning dawned bright and cold and off we all went to our classes. My spirits immediately nose-dived when I discovered that Les Debutantes were not pretty young things in ball gowns but fat, middle-aged German businessmen – it seems that debutantes simply means beginners [just shows how unsuitably named some London debs are!]. Anyway, there we were and having paid for the lesson we had to go through with it.

We persisted with lessons for two full days and during this time spent more time flat on our faces or backsides than on the skis – HOW I longed for my tea tray! Instructions were shouted at us in French, all sorts of terms like "point le poole" and nothing at all about "la plume de ma tante" which is about the limit of my French. All the time as we floundered around cursing in the snow teenage French kids hurtled past us daring each other to get closest to us. We seldom saw our own children but gathered they were learning much faster than we were.

Towards the end of the second day when I had finally and irrevocably decided to hand in my skis and not even bother about a tea tray, something clicked and I progressed down the slope for at least 100 yards without falling over and hardly even a wobble. Life immediately took on new horizons: I gazed at the far peaks and envisaged myself scooting down them with casual nonchalance, I thought how slow the French whiz kids were going – in a day or so I would be overtaking them. I cursed the ski lifts for stopping so early – I could do it! I could ski!

With this new found talent we decided on just one more lesson [there were possibly one or two things we had not quite yet mastered]. Robert, who had outclassed Les Enfants, being a bit older, joined us. No more nursery slopes for us – remember we could ski – and we confidently followed the instructor with a bunch of very inferior Germans to the nearest chairlift.

They all nonchalantly got on and suddenly it was our turn. We had previously never seen people getting onto a chairlift and had NEVER imagined the terror that the operation induced. Robert and I went together, reasoning that as only Pam and the instructor were left, they would come together [a chair takes two]. We shuffled forwards and suddenly the chair whipped round on its cables and cracked us behind the knees causing us to fall into it. It then lurched into space and one glance down was sufficient to freeze my hands both metaphorically and physically onto the side of the chair. The chair swung pendulously a couple of times, I kept my eyes tight shut, screams from below told me to lower my safety bar. This would have meant moving and, worse still, releasing my vice-like grip on the chair, so the action was out of the question. What Robert thought of my behaviour I do not know as he was sitting there quite relaxed and even LEANING FORWARD to point out things of interest far below us. What they were I will never know as after my first terrified glance down I never opened my eyes again.

The agony continued as up and up we went, through clouds, over peaks and valleys. I couldn't feel my arms up to the elbows or legs up to my knees. Robert continued thoroughly to enjoy the whole thing – the fool. Suddenly somewhere near the top of Mont Blanc, a sort of landing stage hove into view, we were going to have to get off or face the prospect of being whipped round the terminus and back down the mountain the way we had come up.

Visions of spending all day on the ruddy thing haunted me. Then, when it did stop at five o'clock, what were the odds on being at one end or the other and not somewhere in between suspended over a crevasse? There were 171 chairs on that lift so the odds were 85 ½ to 1 in favour of being suspended over the crevasse for the night. So one HAD to get off now. Luckily, at this time, I had not heard the story of a friend who, facing a similar predicament, had leapt for it only to get his ski caught in the bottom of the chair and be duly whipped round and headed back down the mountain hanging by one leg like a dead ox at the abattoir.

I opened my eyes, we were nearly there. Our skis touched snow, Robert glided quietly off. I plunged, the chair cracked me in the small of the back, my ski sticks flew from my hand, my balaclava fell over my eyes and I sprawled flat on my face sliding to an ungainly halt at the feet of a crowd of debutantes [German] who howled with laughter. No matter, I was off and nothing, but NOTHING, would ever induce me to get on one of those things again.

The euphoric state of mind at having actually survived this nightmare suddenly changed as a new and grim prospect dawned on me. We were now on the top of Mont Blanc [or so it seemed, actually we were just up the shortest chairlift (ride) some two miles from home] and had to get down. I started taking off my skis prior to sliding down on my bottom. Gone were all last night's grandiose ideas. The slope was almost vertical. One could detect specks at the bottom – probably corpses – and the instructor was gaily setting off with us expected to follow! As my hands and feet were numb from cold and my mind numb from terror I did actually start off after him otherwise I would still be there.

Surprisingly, some feeling started to return. I felt my toes and fingers, blood again coursed through my veins, my mind cleared, some fool fell in front of me – why couldn't the idiot stay up? The wind whistled past my ears, trees whipped by on either side and exhilarating excitement pervaded my system – my God! I was enjoying it. I was really travelling now, over to this side of the piste, turn, back again, straight down, another turn, no point in getting to the bottom of this slope too quickly – only have to wait for all the others to stumble along. A beautiful stem Christie and with breathless triumph I slid to a stop. Robert rose slowly from his reclining position in the snow. "Come on, Father," he said, "let's try and catch up with the rest."

We did go up chairlifts again and even mastered the use of the, button' – a typically French gadget that tows you individually up the slope. You tuck the thing, about the size of a dinner plate, snugly between your legs [if you are a pretty female the lift attendant will help you put it there] and, with a jerk that initially throws you flat on your face, you are towed up the mountain. We all did the 'blue' runs – so called easy, and even ventured onto the occasional 'red' run, [usually by mistake] –slightly more difficult. Black runs were for experts. However, Cousin Anthony scorned even these and being a complete masochist, was only happy being dropped by helicopter at the top of distant peaks and making his way home down vertical slopes through rocks and trees. It appears that to enjoy skiing you have to make yourself totally petrified the entire time. Would I do it again? You bet!

17
Separator

"Is there anything I can get for you while I am in England," I asked.

"Oh! Yes please. If you are anywhere near Norwich, could you bear to get me a washer for my cream separator?"

This seemed a somewhat obscure request as well as a problem. I would have thought such a washer could be obtained much nearer home. 'Home' was a small farm in Zimbabwe and the old girl I was trying to help had been recently widowed but was attempting to carry on running the little dairy farm that she and her late husband had been running in a fairly small way for as long as I could remember.

I was an old friend of the family and was off to England on business. I had called in to see old Liz partly because she would never have forgiven me if I had not and partly because I was genuinely fond of the old girl and knew that she hankered after England but would never be able to afford to go there again. The request, however, took me by surprise.

"Could you not get this washer at the local hardware store?" I ventured.

"Don't be silly," she rejoined, "my separator was made in Norwich and I want a genuine spare part not some local rubbish."

"When did you actually buy the separator?" I probed cautiously.

"Well, sometime before the war I imagine, before we came out here, probably about 1938." It was now 2004 – 66 years ago!

"Where have you been getting spare parts for the separator since then?"

"Haven't needed any, things were made to last in those days."

I was not going anywhere near Norwich but still wanted to help if I could.

"Do you have any sort of address in Norwich which might still stock your washers?"

"I only want one, don't go buying dozens of the things."

"Nevertheless some sort of address would be a help."

"Well, I imagine Caster's are still there, look them up in the book."

"I will do my best," I said meekly and left.

While in London attending to my business I did indeed look up Caster's in the directory and there it was: Caster, Caster and Caster & Co. Ltd. Suppliers of quality dairy equipment etc.

I dialled the number and a frail, old male voice answered.

"Mr. Caster?" I ventured.

"Indeed, how can I help you?" The voice was a little stronger.

"I am over here from Zimbabwe and have been asked by a friend to buy a small part for a cream separator that she purchased from you some time ago."

"Indeed," he said again. "What sort of part may I ask?"

"It is just one washer for a machine bought from you in about 1938," I said rather quickly.

"Ah!" There was a longish pause, then "you do not happen to have any sort of serial number do you?"

"Yes, as a matter of fact I do. It is '00043/37.'"

"Ah!" again. "Just hold on a moment would you?"

The line hummed between my London hotel bedroom and Mr. Caster's office in Norwich. I had made several calls from this room, most of them involving several hundred thousand pounds but now I waited tensely for him to return. Several minutes passed, then the frail old voice came back on the line.

"Yes, I do appear to have a few of those washers still in stock, how many was it you said you wanted?"

"Just the one, actually. How much will it be and how can I pay you?"

"I am afraid I have no idea as to the cost, it is so long since we sold one."

"Well," I said, wanting to conclude the deal, "you cannot buy much with a pound these days, so would that be sufficient?"

"My partners are not here at present," [dead?] "so I cannot discuss it with them but I will unilaterally accept your offer."

"That is very good of you but I am flying back to Zimbabwe in three days' time and if I send the money to you in cash you are unlikely to get it in time for you to mail me the washer, and what about postage?" I did not dare mention 'plastic' for fear of embarrassing the old man.

"That is not a problem," he said, "you just post me a postal order or even two pound notes to cover the postage to Caster, Caster and Caster & Co. [he gave me an address], and I will immediately post you the washer, if you would be good enough to give me your address."

How simple! If only all business could be carried out with this sort of trust. It always used to be, of course, and it usually worked, giving rise to the saying that ' an Englishman's word is his bond'. Clearly Mr. Caster still subscribed to this view and I was inordinately flattered to realise that he assumed I did as well – despite coming from Zimbabwe! The result was that I hurried downstairs with two pound notes and a brief note sealed in an envelope which I asked the receptionist at the desk to post straight away.

Two days later a small package arrived from Norwich. On opening it there was a small metal washer about the size of an old five shilling piece. A day after that I flew back to Zimbabwe with my prize. I regret to say I did not declare it at customs and had no trouble getting it through. The following evening I phoned Liz.

"I got your washer," I said with a note of triumph in my voice.

"What did you pay for it?"

"Well, a pound." I did not dare mention the additional cost of the postage.

"A pound!" she screamed. "You were robbed. Bring it round as soon as you can, would you?"

"Yes," I said meekly and put the phone down.

18
Queuing

Queuing has become a necessary evil in nearly every department of Zimbabwe life these days. I can't bear it. I have an impatient nature and just won't do it unless absolutely essential. The local indigenous population are much better at it than me and seem to accept it as a way of life. At least this is true of the very patient majority who have suffered untold hardships at the hands of a ruling 'elite' over the past few years. This ruling 'elite' have come to believe that they have risen above this boring practice.

The other day I HAD to queue. My doctor had told me to have some X-rays done immediately on my neck for some minor complaint and gave me the address and appointment card for some nearby rooms where this could be done *immediately*.

I approached the desk where a young girl looked at my card, smiled and said, "This will cost you $80, please fill in these forms and take a seat." My heart sank as I viewed a line of some eight or ten other people who had obviously received the same instruction. All were sitting patiently with their noses buried in years' old, crumpled magazines. I duly paid, filled in the forms, sighed, took one of the few remaining chairs and picked up a five year old edition of *South African Rugby* and started thumbing my way through the sticky pages.

Time passed slowly but suddenly there was a general commotion, the door was flung open and a *very* large gentleman, resplendent in a three piece suit, watch chain and the mandatory dark glasses strode up to the desk. Rolls of gleaming fat bulged over his shirt collar and a thin sheen of sweat moistened his brow. He was swinging a bunch of keys which clearly came from a very expensive car. He oozed authority, confidence and the expectation that everyone present would immediately recognise him as one of the ruling 'elite'.

No one said a word but most, including me, stopped reading their less than riveting magazines and watched this deity reach the desk where the little receptionist looked up at him and said, "Good morning sir, how can I help you?"

"I have an appointment with Dr Smithers for an X-ray, I am told it will cost $300 – here it is," he boomed and banged down a wad of brand new US$ notes on the desk. Then added, "And here's another $50 for you, darling, so that I don't have to wait in this queue – I'm a busy man."

The little receptionist carefully counted the $300, put the cash in her drawer, wrote a receipt and pushed it across the counter to the 'busy' man. She paused and then pushed the extra $50 back across the counter as well saying politely, "Thank you sir, but we don't operate that way here, please take a seat."

All of us who had been reading grotty magazines were now gazing fascinated at this little unfolding tableau. For myself – I wanted to applaud loudly, rush up and kiss the little receptionist!

Current member of the ruling 'elite' was not quite so impressed. Actually he was lost for words. To give him his due though he tried to speak but all that emerged from his mouth was a high-pitched squeak and a thin dribble of spittle. He waved his arms in the air and, in so doing, dropped the keys to the very expensive car onto the highly polished floor of the reception area. He stood for a moment breathing heavily and then tried to speak again. This time he succeeded, "You'll hear more about this," he screamed [spittle flying in all directions] and turned to storm out of the building.

He got no further than the door when he remembered the keys to the very expensive car – Mercedes, obviously! – which he had dropped on the floor. Mustering all the dignity he could, he strode back into the building and, locating the said keys on the floor, stopped and wanted to pick them up. Now I have told you that he was very large, but out of respect for one of the ruling 'elite', I omitted to say that he was also very fat. Well, he was and as such was totally unable to bend this large [fat] frame to the required angle that would enable him to reach the keys. He tried by putting one fat leg as far backwards as he could and leaning forward – his large girth prevented him from actually bending. This manoeuvre was dangerous on a highly polished floor and as he made a frantic grab for the keys, his foot slipped and he crashed to the ground. In struggling to rise from his most undignified position he stood on and crushed the remote control attached to the keys which was needed to open his car door.

He was eventually helped to his feet by one of my fellow queuers who obviously thought he would earn a few 'Brownie Points' by assisting so eminent a personage, who now stood, breathing heavily, and looking sadly at the squashed remote in his hand which clearly would not now open the door of his expensive car. Again mustering what dignity he could and ignoring the suppressed mirth of us all, he approached the little receptionist again. "My cell phone is in my car which I cannot now open so ring the Zimoco garage headquarters immediately and tell them to send an engineer here straight away to open the car," he blustered.

"Certainly sir," said the little receptionist, "we do charge $1 to make local calls though." A dollar coin was banged down on the desk and 'member of the ruling elite' stood glaring at the little receptionist. "Thank you sir," she said, "please take a seat."

I did not mind queuing one bit that day – not one little bit!

19
Spring

What is really meant by 'Spring'? I have given it a capital 'S' here but I don't think it deserves to have one. In any of the nine meanings listed in Collins Pocket English Dictionary they are all small. Most times it is used there is an article of sorts in front of it, as in a spring, when referring to a source of bubbling water, or a coiled spring, when referring to a coiled spring! You can also spring into the air or you can search round for someone to help spring you from prison but these last are verbs and not nouns. A boiler can spring a leak and I am not sure quite what the word is classified as then, still a verb I suppose.

However, if you just say, spring, or even the spring, with or without a capital 'S', most people will assume that you are speaking about a certain time of year. But this in itself is confusing – what time of year? If you are speaking to an Australian and tell him that you will meet up again this spring he will think it might well be at the Melbourne Cup in November. I am writing this in England so when I speak of spring most people will know I am referring to one of the two or three months at the end of winter, our winter, when the weather briefly becomes a bit warmer – sort of June or July in my limited experience!

Whenever it does occur it is usually a time of rejoicing – all sorts of reasons spring to mind. If you live in England I think that my main memories are of wild flowers. Nervous little snowdrops appear first, but it is really still winter when they so bravely peep out of the frost hardened earth. Still, it is a sign of better things to come and their lead is followed by daffodils, crocuses, primroses and bluebells etc. Then of course there are young animals. Little lambs springing about all over the place, cattle sprung from their winter hibernation and into meadows flushed with buttercups and dandelions amid a sea of green grass. Bare hedges suddenly sprouting little green shoots, trees get their leaves back again, birds start sitting on eggs – but we can't really see this as they are hidden in the newly clothed hedges and trees. In short, life returns to the English countryside. This annual miracle has been written about in prose and poetry many times by far more able pens than mine so I am not about to compete with the likes of Mr Wordsworth who bangs on about daffodils and things ad infinitum.

But I have lived most of my life in Africa, south of the equator. Days and nights there in the tropics are not as dramatically different from here in England and the limited twilight only varies by an hour or so. The main reason why spring is looked forward to in Africa is pretty much the opposite of why the English cherish it. In England we long for the sun, warm weather and less rain. In Africa we longed for cooler weather and, above all, *rain*! Rain to bring the parched earth back to life, rain to get the water courses running again, rain so that farmers could start planting their crops. There would have been a long dry six months with no rain, so the countryside would be parched and tinder dry, the air hazy with smoke from a hundred grass fires and a trail of dust behind any vehicle. Dams would be dry, boreholes maybe just holding out, cattle thin and unhappy and farmers gazing daily at the sky in the hope of seeing some sort of cloud build-up. Streaks of distant lightning would be the first sign that some relief from the searing heat was on its way, rumbles of thunder and a few big, black, lovely clouds. Then maybe a few heavy drops bouncing back off the hard earth raising a little dust as they landed but all too soon they would stop and within an hour there would be no trace of any rain having fallen.

Wild animals probably look forward to an African spring as much as anybody;. the dry months having made life progressively harder and harder for them. They will have had to search further and further afield for their food, which in itself would have burnt off much needed fat and energy. The elephant needs about 500lbs of food a day, the hippo emerges from its daytime water home to eat grass and most antelope rely also entirely on grass for their food, as do buffalo, wildebeest and zebra. Browsing animals, including some of the other larger antelope, giraffe and the few remaining rhinos need green shoots on the scrub bushes. Grass and green shoots do not grow without rain.

One of Africa's most common and most beautiful antelope is the impala and they are able to retain their young in the womb until there is enough green grass to feed themselves and their new babies, so spring is a vital time for them.

What about the carnivores though? They probably do not like spring. In the dry season there is very restricted water so game can easily be ambushed near the few remaining waterholes where they must congregate and their prey is weaker and easier to catch because it is short of food. Spring puts an end to all that. There is water everywhere and their prey become much more scattered.

So this is a very brief description of how I see spring when it is a season of the year. I remember many springs particularly in Africa when our very livelihood depended upon rain falling at the right time – in the spring. On my farm in Zimbabwe it used to be due in late October and it usually started in the form of a huge storm, more often than not in the late afternoon. I remember on many occasions driving back to the farm from a visit to our nearest town and seeing a build-up of clouds over our area and willing them to be over my farm. As the road twisted and turned one got differing angles as to where the clouds were in relation to the farm and one's spirits either soared or plummeted depending on where you thought the clouds were. If you suddenly realised that your farm was going to miss out completely but that your neighbour was getting a lovely heavy storm, irrationally you hated him – why should he *always* get the rain and not me?

As October turned into November I would become more desperate. One morning my new wife who was fresh out from England threw back the bedroom curtains to reveal yet another of Africa's glorious, sparkling, cloudless dawns. "Oh, what a lovely morning!" she exclaimed as I lay snuggled up in bed, unable to see out of the window. "Does that mean it is pouring with rain?" I asked, full of hope. So even a glorious spring morning means different things to different people.

So what was my favourite spring? I will tell you.

It was in Zimbabwe and spring was late – as usual. My cows had started calving as I had planned they should, in late October to catch the new grass. But there was no new grass and, not having the ability of the impala to retain their babies until there was, they dropped their calves anyway. This meant expensive food had to be bought in for the new mothers. It also meant that all the cows and calves tended to congregate in one place so as to receive this feed. This led to a lot of weak little calves wandering around in an open space and not hidden away as mother cows normally do with their newborn calves.

Suddenly we started losing calves. One morning a mother cow came for her feed but was not really interested in eating it, she just wandered around bellowing. Where was her calf, as this was clearly the problem? We searched the area and soon came across a half-eaten carcass of a small black calf. Obviously killed by some fairly large predator what could it be? The choice was limited – leopard, hyena, wild dog, jackal or just maybe, cheetah. We scoured the surrounding area for spoor but, as it was so dry, we could not really find anything significant.

Next morning it was the same story. Another young cow – a heifer with her first calf was very agitated and obviously desperate to find her new baby. We soon found it some distance away and again no more than half-eaten. This was getting serious. We organised an extensive search of the whole area and in a damp patch of earth near a water trough there was a very clear set of foot prints. Paw prints, or spoor would probably be a more accurate description. We all bent down and my herdsman, his assistant, my wife and I all gazed at what we assumed was the spoor of the offending calf killer.

"Leopard," said my wife.

"Hyena," said the herdsman.

"Wild dog," I said.

"Cheetah," whispered the herdsman's assistant.

Animated discussion followed. "It can't be any kind of cat," I pointed out, "you can clearly see the claw marks and cats withdraw their claws so it can't be a leopard." My wife looked both disappointed and glad at the same time. She loves leopards and would have been very excited at the thought of one of these lovely animals being on the farm, but glad that her favourite animal was being ruled out as a suspect of this crime.

"So it must be a hyena or a wild dog," said the herdsman. "You can always see the claws in their spoor."

The assistant herdsman was quite young and new to the job so was reluctant to push himself forward, however with a little cough he did say quite quietly, "A cheetah is indeed a cat but it is the only cat that cannot retract its claws. This spoor is much too small for a hyena, wild dogs nearly always hunt in packs and very seldom leave anything of what they have just killed so I still say it is a cheetah."

The herdsman was pretty put out by being shown up by his underling, "There has not been a cheetah seen in these parts for years now, Justin, and where do you think you have suddenly acquired all this knowledge?"

"Before getting employment here I worked with a gang of poachers in the Mana Pools National Park," said Justin with a little chuckle, "I knew this was a bad thing to do so I left them – but I did learn a lot. This spoor comes from a cheetah. I am not saying the cheetah killed the calves but it did have a drink of water here."

This was a long speech for the youngster and I admired his courage in admitting where he had learned about tracking. He had a point. The spoor was not large at all so certainly not a hyena and what Justin had said about wild dogs was true enough. So what to do now? I sat in a tree near where we fed the cattle most of the next night armed with a .256 rifle. But as I could see nothing and any self-respecting predator would very soon get my scent anyway, it was not a wild success. I neither saw nor heard anything and was cold, tired and bad-tempered by 3 o'clock in the morning so retired to bed where I made my wife cold and bad-tempered as well.

Next morning I did not want to insult my head herdsman by consulting his underling in front of him so waited until he had gone off to inspect the weaner herd and collared young Justin.

"How would your poacher friends catch or kill this cheetah or whatever it is that is killing my calves?" I asked him.

He was silent for a few minutes, then just said, "A spring trap."

"What is a spring trap?" I asked, feeling a little stupid at asking advice from my youngest and newest employee.

"You make a cage with two separate compartments. In the rear compartment you put a goat. You then leave the front of the cage open and attach a spring to the floor. When the cheetah enters the cage to try and kill the goat it treads on the floor and the spring releases the door which slams down and captures it alive." Another long speech from Justin but he seemed very confident.

So I got just such a cage as he had suggested made in our own workshop. It was a bit fiddly making the spring attachment from the floor to the door which would slide down behind anything entering the cage but it did seem to work. We already had a few goats and they were excellent bait as they could be guaranteed to make a lot of noise all night and hopefully attract the cheetah. Not nice for the goat but it would be perfectly safe in its own little compartment.

No further calf had been killed in the couple of days that it had taken to make the cage and we were beginning to hope that whatever had been killing them had gone away but Justin said that if the cheetah had eaten two nights running, as it had, it would very likely not feed again for a few nights. So we put the cage out in the area where we had been feeding the cows and inserted a very reluctant goat who immediately obliged by objecting very strongly to the role we were forcing it to play, in that it emitted a string of very loud, pathetic bleats. "Just keep that up," I said as we all left the scene.

We could hear nothing from our house so we all approached the cage next morning as soon as it got light. While still some 50 yards away we were electrified to hear a low growl. Wow!! In the cage was a very unhappy goat and – a young cheetah. Our excitement was intense and everybody talked at once. One question finally emerged from this and that was, what now?

I have already told you that my wife's favourite animal is a leopard but a very close second comes a cheetah so I had to tread very carefully in deciding the fate of the killer of my calves. Suffice it to say that no decision was reached that day. We released a very relieved goat and dragged the cage containing a pretty angry cheetah into the garden of our house and there it spent the night while debate raged inside the house as to its fate.

"It is a proven calf killer and must be shot," was the basis of my argument.

"You can't possibly kill a lovely, rare animal like that," was the case for the defence, eloquently put by my wife and supported by my teenage daughter.

Various compromise solutions were aired well into the night but we eventually went to bed not really speaking to each other and our goodnight kiss was frosty to say the least.

Next morning there was a freshly killed, half-eaten calf.

I summoned Justin and wordlessly pointed to the pathetic little carcass.

"It must be a jackal," he said.

"Jackal! Kill a calf, no," said I.

"Oh yes, a newborn calf is very easy prey for a full-grown male jackal. See, it has eaten a lot so will not be far away. Get the dogs, bring your shotgun and we will soon find it."

I was now actually taking orders from the youngest and newest of my employees but again he did have a point. So I collected our motley assortment of dogs and armed with SSG in my 12 bore shotgun set off with Justin to find a fat, overfed jackal.

To cut this story about spring a bit short, suffice it to say that very soon we found the culprit and I despatched it in quick time. A post-mortem examination revealed without any doubt that it was indeed the killer.

So, the case for the prosecution against the imprisoned cheetah now collapsed like a pack of cards. But the problem of what to do with it remained unsolved.

More debate raged, tempers rose and the cheetah got hungry and thirsty. My daughter was the first to do anything sensible and pushed a bowl of water and a dead chicken into the cage. To our surprise the cheetah stopped growling, lapped up the water and, as we walked away, got stuck into the chicken.

Of all wild animals the cheetah has, over many years, proved to be the most amenable to being domesticated; indeed if caught young they make pets akin to domestic dogs. This cheetah was probably the equivalent of a teenager and as such seemed to take to my teenage daughter. Quite where it had come from we never discovered but before too long we released it from the cage and it became my daughter's devoted pet.

Rain fell the morning after we shot the jackal, no more calves were killed, the grass grew long and green and we had the best season since moving onto the farm.

Our beloved cheetah needed a name. It had been caught in a spring trap in spring so there really was only one name for it and Spring [with a capital S!] was an adored pet for many years to come.

20
The Little Impala – a Children's Story

An impala is a bit like an English deer but it lives in Africa and is called an antelope. It is very beautiful. It has a lovely soft, brown, shiny coat, huge eyes with long lashes and long, thin legs which are really very strong. The daddy impala has long curving horns with sharp points at the end and he uses them to protect his herd. The mummy impalas do not have any horns; they do not need them because they do not have to fight. They love to run and jump – particularly jump because they are very good at it and go high in the air.

The daddy impala is the only male in the herd and he has about thirty wives – imagine that! Thirty wives! They keep him very busy but he looks after them all very well and sees that they always have plenty of nice grass to eat.

This can be difficult because Africa is a very hot country and if it does not rain often the grass does not grow properly so the impalas can get hungry. As this can happen quite often the mummy impalas have become very clever and do not have their babies until they can see lovely green shoots of grass growing well after good rain. This usually happens at about the same time each year, in November, so it is a very important month to the impala herd.

Now there was one herd of impalas that lived on a big farm owned by an old farmer who loved his animals. He had lots of cows, lots of horses, a few sheep and some goats as well as rabbits, chickens, ducks, geese, turkeys and one donkey. All these animals ate lots of grass but usually there was still enough for the impalas to have some as well and the farmer liked having the impalas on his farm. The farmer also grew a crop called maize and he used this to help feed his animals when the rain was not as good as he had hoped. The farmer could not make any money out of the impalas as they were just wild animals, but he could milk the cows and goats, ride the horses and sell the wool from the sheep as well as collect eggs from his chickens and ducks while his children rode the donkey. But he liked the impalas so was happy to have them share his grass.

One November it rained as usual and all the impala mummies had their babies as planned and the daddy was very proud. The first shoots of grass were sweet and tender and the mummies all ate it so that they could produce good milk for their babies. All the other animals on the farm were also enjoying the new grass [except the donkey, which had a tummy ache from eating too many carrots] and the farmer was happy. But, as sometimes happens in Africa, the lovely rain that had made the grass grow suddenly stopped and it got drier and drier. The tender green shoots started to curl up in the heat and were no longer good to eat. The mummy impalas' milk started to stop coming and the babies became hungry and stopped growing properly. The daddy impala became very worried and wondered what he could do to get some proper food.

All the farmer's animals were getting hungry as well [particularly the donkey as there were no carrots either], so the farmer had to spend a lot of money and buy some hay. The animals would much rather have had the lovely green grass to eat instead of the dry hay but it was better than nothing – and the impalas had nothing. But there was hope in sight. The farmer had made a deep hole in the ground called a borehole and had put a pipe down this hole and could pump water up from deep down in the earth. He used this water to keep his maize alive and make it grow strong so soon there would be some grain that he could give his animals as well and also feed the maize plant to them. In the field where the maize was, the plants were lovely and green and looked so very different from the horrid dried up brown grass which was everywhere else.

The impala herd was getting thinner and thinner until one day the youngest baby died of hunger. He – it was a little boy – had been born last and his mummy had never had any nice green grass to eat after he had been born so he had never had any nice rich milk. The big daddy impala ram was very upset about this and decided to go off on his own and just see if there was any nice green grass anywhere.

His search brought him to the edge of the farmer's field and, peeping over the fence, he saw row after row of lovely, juicy, green plants. Just a few mouthfuls of those would help the milk of all the mummies of my babies, he thought, and then no more of them would die. He hurried back to where the herd was waiting in the shade of some thorn trees so that they could keep out of the blazing hot sun.

Impalas cannot really talk like we do but in 'impala language' he told his wives what he had discovered and said that when it got cooler in the evening they would all move off to the maize field. They were all very excited at the thought of getting some lovely green food to eat after so long with none.

When they got to the field they found there was a small fence all the way round it but if there is one thing impalas can do well it is jump; they do it often just for fun and can jump really high so it was no problem jumping into the field and even some of the quite small babies managed to do it easily.

In the field they found rows and rows of lovely green maize shoots which were still quite small but very delicious. Each shoot was not much more than a mouthful for the hungry mummy impalas so they each needed to eat a lot of them to fill their empty tummies. They all ate so much that it was even a little bit difficult for them to jump the fence out of the field. But as they are such good jumpers it was not really a problem and afterwards they went back to their own area and slept for a bit. In the morning all the mummy impalas had lovely creamy milk and the thin little babies were at last able to drink their fill and even those which were small and ill soon started feeling strong and well.

This should be the happy ending of this story but very sadly it is not. Next morning the farmer went down to his maize field to put more water on as usual and was horrified to see that most of the lovely green maize shoots had been nibbled off and so the plants would now die however much water he put on. It was easy for him to see who had eaten all the little shoots, as in the damp soil there were lots of tiny footprints and these could only have been made by the impalas. He was very, very angry and very, very worried. If he could not grow a proper crop of maize all his animals might die.

The little eaten shoots would not grow any more so if he was to get a crop he had to plant more seeds. This was a lot of work and cost a lot of money which he had to borrow from a wicked bank manager. Now he had to pay this money back when the maize was big and he would have to sell some of it to do this so there would be less to feed his animals. He was very worried indeed and one day when his children had gone to school, he even sold the donkey so there was one less mouth to feed. They were very sad when they came home and found no donkey.

He pumped water onto the newly planted seeds and soon tiny little shoots appeared above the wet soil and he hoped that he still might get a decent crop of maize. One evening he was returning later than usual from his field when suddenly he saw all the impalas creeping out of the bushes and heading towards his field. The daddy impala had been watching what was happening in the field and knew that there were some more little green shoots. The mummy impalas and their babies were hungry again so he had planned another raid on the maize field. The farmer was furious. "If those impalas get into my field again they will eat all those lovely young shoots and I will have no maize at all this year," he thought.

He then did a terrible thing. He rushed back to his house and got out his gun and went back to where he had seen the impalas. They had crept much closer to the field by now and were even about to jump in and begin eating the maize. I am afraid to say that the farmer needed no more proof of what could happen and he opened fire on them. It was horrid. The daddy impala was killed straight away as he was the leader and a lot of the mummies were killed as well and even some of the babies. All the rest turned round and ran and ran and ran until they were far, far away from the field, the farmer and the farmer's beastly gun.

Some of the babies had no mothers now as they had been shot and they soon died of hunger and even the mummies that had not been shot could not feed their babies properly as there was no nice grass where they ran to and ALL the babies died. It was terrible as now the whole lovely herd only had a very few thin mummy impalas left and even they had a very hard life trying to stay alive in the new place that they had run to and no daddy impala to look after them.

The farmer, back at the maize field, was very sorry for what he had done but hoped he would now have a good crop and could feed his own animals and perhaps even buy the donkey back as his children were very sad not to have it. Next morning he went back to the field to start the pump to put water on the maize and after doing this, he was just about to leave to go back to his house for breakfast, when he saw a small movement in the grass near to the place where he had shot the impalas last night. He took a closer look and there, lying in some long, dry grass was a tiny, thin, very unhappy baby boy impala. It looked up at him as he got near and one huge tear ran down its face from a huge dark eye.

The farmer felt very, very sorry for the poor little animal and, not really realising what he was doing, bent down and picked him up. The poor little impala snuggled against him and made a sweet little grunt. "What shall I do now?" thought the farmer. What he did was to take the poor little thing home and hand him over to his wife and children to look after. It was a funny thing to do after shooting so many of the baby impala's relations, wasn't it? But the farmer was not really a cruel man and he loved all animals.

His children were very excited at having such a sweet little animal to look after and spent a lot of time every day seeing that he was made comfortable and had plenty of milk to drink. "As we do not have a donkey to look after now we can look after Pala instead," they said, "and he is so small that he will not eat nearly as much as the donkey, so it is alright to keep him."

So they did keep him and quite soon he grew into a very handsome young ram. His horns started growing and he learned to run round the garden and jump and jump and jump because he felt so well and happy. It was a good time for the farmer as well because the rain fell, the sun shone and the grass all grew back again and the maize all grew tall and good without having to put water on it.

But what had happened to the poor impala mummies that had run so far away? There were only a few left and it took a long time for them to get well again as the place they had run to was not very nice and the little bits of grass were sour and horrid. So after the good rain they plucked up their courage and went back to their old home on the farmer's farm. Here the grass was sweet and good just like it used to be and slowly they got fat and well again. But one very serious thing was missing – there was no daddy impala so they had no leader or a daddy for any more babies.

Pala, for that was the name of the little impala that was now a very big impala, was happy living in the garden of the farmer and being looked after by his children. He had made friends with the dogs, the cat and even a fat pig that also lived in the garden but none of these were impalas and Pala longed to meet some animals the same as him. As he was fully grown now he was not locked up anywhere and at night he just slept under a bush in the garden.

One very quiet night he was dozing under his bush when he heard a funny noise in the distance. He stood up and walked to the edge of the garden. He had never heard a noise quite like this but somehow he knew what it was. It was the noise that a herd of impalas make when they are frightened. Without thinking anymore, Pala jumped over the small garden fence and galloped towards the sound. It did not take him very long to arrive at the area where he had been born and to which the remains of the impala herd had recently returned. As he rounded a corner he nearly ran straight into four or five mummy impalas which were making their frightened noise and looking over their shoulders. They were running very fast because close behind them, making excited little yapping noises, were three wild dogs. Wild dogs are very good hunters and love eating impalas. Although the mummy impalas were running very fast the wild dogs were running a little bit faster and it was looking very dangerous for the last of the mummy impalas which was getting tired.

Now Pala was not running away, he was actually running towards both the mummy impalas and the wild dogs. Remember he had never even seen another impala but somehow he knew these were his relations. He had never seen a wild dog either but he knew for certain that these were the enemies of the impalas. So as the mummy impalas rushed past him and he saw the first wild dog about to catch the last one, he lowered his head and with his great big horns sticking out in front of him he charged the leading wild dog.

Wild dogs are used to chasing impalas and never had they been charged by one. The leading wild dog did not really know what to do so he jumped to one side and ran off into the bush. The other ones following close behind followed him and then they all stopped running and sat down with their tongues hanging out and panting loudly. I think they were also shaking their heads and wondering how an impala had suddenly chased them!

Meanwhile the mummy impalas were really out of breath as well but kept on running a bit until they were safely away from the wild dogs. Then they stopped too and I think they were shaking their heads as well. Who on earth was that lovely, big, brave daddy impala that has saved us all from the wild dogs was what they were all thinking. What a hero! What a leader he would make! Where has he gone? We must find him.

Now Pala did not really know how brave he had been. Suddenly there was no one in front of him and he was all alone. So he stopped and I think he was shaking his head as well. He knew the wild dogs were dangerous but where were those lovely animals that they had been chasing. Who were they? He must find them. So he turned round and trotted back the way he had come. The wild dogs that were now lying down in the shade saw him coming and hurried away. They did not want to be chased again by those huge horns. Pala trotted on and it was not long before he came up to the mummy impalas who were all in a little bunch talking impala talk to each other and wondering where their saviour had got to. Suddenly they looked up and there he was – trotting towards them, with his magnificent head held high and coat gleaming in the moonlight. What a sight he was!

Pala trotted right up to them and stopped. All the mummy impalas started talking at once and Pala was amazed that he could understand every word. "These are my family," he realised, "I must stay with them always and look after them because I have horns and they do not." Impalas do not really have parties like we do, but everyone was very, very happy and they all ran off together back to their special area doing big jumps of joy all the way.

Next morning, back at the farmhouse, the children ran into the garden to say 'good morning' to Pala. They did not give him milk now as he was too big but they always brought him something like bread, a little maize or some cabbage leaves. But where was he? They called and called and looked everywhere. At last they ran back into the house, very worried, and told their parents. Now the farmer was a very wise man and he soon guessed what had happened and explained to his children that wild animals usually go back to the wild when they are grown-up and this is probably what Pala had done.

Later the farmer drove out to the place where he knew the impalas used to live and there, with just eight mummy impalas, he saw Pala. Pala was looking very proud and just stood there looking at his friend, the farmer, but all the mummy impalas ran away as they remembered the last time they had seen the farmer when he had his gun. The farmer just grinned and said, "You just stay there, Pala, with your new wives and we will remain friends forever."

Well, Pala did stay in that area with his new wives and when the next rainy season was over and the new grass was shooting from the earth a whole lot of sweet little baby impalas were born. They ran and jumped in the sunshine and the mummies were very pleased and Pala was very proud.

So this could also be the end of the story because the farmer and his family were very happy as well and had even bought the donkey back again, with money from last year's very good maize crop. But, as often happens in Africa, the rains the following season were no good at all. A little bit of grass did grow and a new crop of little baby impalas were born, so the herd was getting bigger again, but then no more rain fell and the green shoots all died and the mummy impalas' milk dried up and the babies got thinner and thinner, just like last time. Pala became very worried as it was now his job to look after the herd and so he called a meeting. In Impala language he told his wives that he knew that his friend the farmer had a big field and in it he was pumping water onto lovely little juicy, green shoots of maize and this was just what the mummy impalas needed to make milk for the babies, so he planned to take them to the field that very evening.

Oh dear! "No, no, no," said all the mummy impalas at once, "we will all be shot if we do that – like last time – don't you remember?"

Pala had been such a tiny baby when that had happened many years before that of course he did not remember. He just remembered being looked after by a kind farmer and his family. He still wanted to go and eat the maize but his wives, the mummy impalas, refused to go with him. "Well all our babies will die if we just stay here," he said.

The mummy impalas were very unhappy and very sad but they would not go. Then one morning when all of them were feeling very hungry and the babies were getting sicker and sicker, there was a rumbling in the distance and suddenly a tractor came into view and it was pulling a cart. The farmer was driving the tractor and when he saw the impala herd he stopped. Then he climbed onto the cart and with a long fork started throwing out lovely green lucerne onto the ground. Lucerne is a delicious type of green grass and the farmer had grown it especially with water from his pump for his cows and now he was giving some of it to the impalas. Wasn't that a very kind thing to do?

And every day he brought a small load out to them so that the mummies got fat and well and had lots of milk so the babies also got fat and well and grew up into more lovely impalas. And Pala? Well, he became the proudest impala father there had ever been and soon had a lovely herd of thirty wives. It was a very good thing that he had listened to what his wives told him, wasn't it? So that really is the end of the story as they all lived happily ever after. Even the donkey!

21
The Genuine Hunter

Sandy Birbeck loved life – and so he should. He was born into a wealthy North Yorkshire family [although some say that with a name like that he should have been born in Norfolk]; was educated at all the best schools [if you can call Eton 'one of the best schools'], spent a 'gap year' in Africa, went on to Cambridge University, travelled a bit more in Argentina where he played a lot of polo, Australia where he drank a lot of beer and France where he chased a lot of girls.

When he was not doing all this he went home, played cricket for the village in the summer, shot a vast amount of birds, hunted and skied in the winter. By the time he was 25 he felt he should do a bit of work – so did his father! Sandy was actually no fool and soon joined a small company in the City of London together with university friends which was specialising in the founding of a service for sending e-mails which was then referred to as a 'Dot Com' company. E-mails had been around for a bit but the general public were just beginning to cotton on to this marvellous new way of communicating and Sandy's company cashed in hugely.

As the eldest son and due to inherit the family estate, Sandy was not exactly short of the old 'folding stuff' but suddenly he found himself rich beyond his [or his father's] wildest dreams. He was a millionaire several times over by any form of calculation. Much as he enjoyed his work, he enjoyed his leisure even more and with so much money now at his disposal he saw no real reason not to indulge in these leisure pursuits.

But where to start? At least three weeks skiing in Austria sometime after the home shooting season ended. As much grouse shooting as possible between mid-August and November. A little pheasant shooting perhaps, but he did not really enjoy having vast flocks of semi-tame birds flopping over his head – he wanted the real thing. Polo in the summer, yes, and he would hire some high goal professionals from Argentina to ensure that he played at a decent level. They could bring him some of their lovely Criollo ponies as well to see that he was well mounted. Hunting had to be fitted in somewhere – almost certainly between Christmas and the spring.

That all looked pretty good but at least six weeks a year had to be set aside for his one real passion – Big Game hunting in Africa. He had done very little but enough to appreciate the adrenalin rush of following a buffalo into thick bush or getting the first glimpse of a leopard coming to the bait. He could now afford to hire the best professional hunters and visit the very best places. The 'Big Five' were some hunters' dream of shooting, namely elephant, lion, buffalo, leopard and rhino. Sandy was happy about the first four but did not want a rhino – even then in the 1970s rhino, particularly the black rhino, was becoming very scarce due to poaching.

So for the next ten years Sandy religiously went to Africa for a good six weeks of hunting – not galloping around on horses but tracking through the African bush. He hired the best professional hunters who used to be called 'White Hunters' for some obscure reason – probably because they were white! These hunters had the best trackers and Sandy soon learned a lot about the fascinating art of tracking game in thick bush or anywhere else for that matter.

Sandy was not a butcher; he enjoyed the hunt as much as the actual result. He did do a little shooting for the pot on these safaris but mostly restricted himself to trying to obtain the best possible trophy. There was, of course, a lot of game other than big game and over the years he got some excellent trophies of things like greater kudu, sable, eland, nyala, sitatunga and zebra. But his passion remained for the big stuff and from these he wanted only the very best trophy – something that could preferably be listed in Rowland Ward's book of the biggest and best trophies ever shot.

In Northern Namibia around the Kaokoveld area he got an exceptionally big lion which, despite it not having an outstanding mane, he had stuffed and mounted in its entirety and positioned in the hall of the stately pile that he had recently moved into on the death of his father. The Selous area of central Tanzania provided the elephant. This had taken a number of safaris before he was satisfied that anything with tusks over 100 lbs each was very, very rare these days, so he settled for a magnificent pair of almost symmetrical tusks weighing 92 and 97 lbs each. The hunt had been long and difficult for this wily old boy who had survived the best efforts of several previous hunters over many years.

A leopard is always a very worthy opponent and it was actually on private land in the Mkushi district of Zambia that Sandy finally added a fine old male to his growing collection. This particular trophy pleased him more than most as the animal in question had been terrorising the local Africans for months and had eaten a large number of their goats and sheep.

There remained only a really good buffalo to complete Sandy's 'Big Four'. He had hunted buffalo on several occasions but never found a bull that quite measured up to his exacting standard. This would be his ultimate prize as he rated the buffalo as the most dangerous and worthy of opponents.

"When I do get a real beauty I may just stop hunting these magnificent animals and take up photography," he told his new bride – much to her relief.

Sandy was over 40 by now and should have been in the prime of life. He still had enough money to ensure that he would never really have to work again – except to run the ancestral estate, of course. He had a lovely, adoring wife, a young son and heir together with a cheeky little daughter. What more could a man want? Health. Sandy had always been pretty fit, what with all the outdoor sport that he indulged in, but suddenly he started losing weight and getting cramping pains at the bottom of his stomach.

He visited the family doctor and after a series of tests from him and a variety of specialists, the result he had been dreading was revealed. He had cancer of the colon.

"We can keep it at bay for quite a long time, old boy, but long term prospects are honestly not that good," said the doctor, who knew his patient would want him to be totally honest.

They did keep it at bay and when his great friend Tony Smith-Riley, a professional hunter, wrote to him asking what his hunting plans were he replied that, yes, he would like a three week hunting safari in the Zambezi valley of Zimbabwe. The Zambezi had always been his favourite river and the hunting areas downstream from Mana Pools were famous for its buffalo. And it was buffalo that he wanted to hunt on what he was pretty certain would be his last safari.

Katherine, his wife, was very against the whole idea but sensibly knew it would be no good trying to deter him so agreed to the plan with as good a grace as possible. She would not be travelling with him.

So it was that in late September he flew to Harare and was met by Tony. They only spent one night at Meikles hotel before driving the 300 odd miles north to the Zambezi. A camp had already been set up on a lovely site on the banks of the mighty river looking across to the escarpment in Zambia on the other side.

They arrived soon after lunch and, after a quick siesta, Sandy said he would like to take the shotgun and walk along the banks of the river just absorbing the beauty of the place and perhaps getting a shot at a guinea fowl or francolin which would make a welcome addition to the larder.

Normally Tony, as the professional hunter, would have gone with him but there were jobs to do round the camp and he knew Sandy was a very experienced bushman and would have no difficulty looking after himself so he remained in camp and Sandy walked off on his own, revelling in the sheer magnificence of the river and the sounds of the African bush.

He had walked perhaps a mile or so when, with a flurry of wings and loud squawk, a couple of francolin rose from a nearby patch of thick reeds. Francolin are easier to shoot than grouse and Sandy had no difficulty in dropping them both.

He never saw them fall to the ground though. At the sound of the first shot there burst from the same clump of reeds the biggest buffalo bull that Sandy had ever seen. Its flanks were covered in mud and on top of the huge head were a magnificent set of gleaming black horns hanging low down beside the bull's face before curving up again in an almost symmetrical sweep. They were huge.

Sandy just stood there transfixed as the bull snorted and lumbered off into some thick *jesse bush*. He felt he had never seen anything quite so magnificent in all his experience. In a daze, and forgetting all about the francolin, he hurriedly retraced his steps back to camp. He knew already that he wanted that bull like he had wanted nothing else in his hunting life. What a wonderful trophy to complete his collection on possibly his last hunt. The blank space in the library at home would be filled at last.

Tony believed Sandy's story. Sandy was not prone to exaggeration, he knew what he was speaking about and his obvious excitement was contagious. Clearly there was no time to do anything that evening, the sun was already sinking behind the Zambian hills, but at first light next morning Sandy, Tony and Tony's old Wakamba tracker, Wambua, were on their way along the riverbank to follow the tracks of the old bull.

The going was tough. September is towards the end of the dry season in Zimbabwe and the sun burned down, the tsetse flies were very busy and the tracks were difficult to follow even for an experienced tracker like Wambua. After three hours the three stopped for a quick rest and drink of water. At about one o' clock they stopped again for something to eat. Sandy was not feeling that good but refused to say anything.

Round about three o'clock they were about to give up for the day and start the long trek back to camp when Wambua suddenly held up his hand, then motioned them to squat down. Glancing round at them, he pointed back over his shoulder. Sandy could see nothing but as Wambua started to creep forward he did suddenly detect a darker form in the bush ahead. But in looking up he stumbled slightly and in doing so trod on a dry twig which snapped with a bang like a mini pistol shot. The dark form ahead exploded into life and the three of them watched in frustration as the object of the day's hunt quickly disappeared deeper into the bush.

"Well, that's it for today," said Tony trying to hide his annoyance and they started the long, tiring walk back to camp.

Sandy was frankly exhausted when they did get back. OK, it had been a very long day and he had only arrived in the country a couple of days ago. Also he knew that he had been the cause of the hunt failing but he used to take this sort of thing in his stride.

He felt better next morning when they boarded the Land Rover and drove as near as they could get to where they had lost the bull the day before. They picked up the spoor easily enough and were making good progress until the bull turned up into the hills and over some very rocky ground. Wambua was amazing and followed minute signs that neither of the other two could even see but by four o'clock they were all on their knees, covered in tsetse fly bites and far from camp.

It was after dark when they finally slumped into the camp chairs and Mwangi, the cook, tactfully put a large glass of whisky into the hands of Sandy and Tony while Wambua slunk off to his own fire.

"If we are ever going to get this cunning old bastard, we will have to sleep on the trail," said Tony." "It's a total waste of time coming back here every night. Are you up to it? You look buggered. Nothing wrong, I hope?"

"I'm fine, Tony," replied Sandy rather too quickly, "I'll do whatever you say. Just get me a shot at that bull."

So it was that before dawn next morning the three of them plus a driver loaded iron rations for three days into the 'landy' and set off to the area where they had lost the trail the night before. Here they disembarked and sent the vehicle back to camp with the driver as they had no idea where they would be three days hence.

The next three days were certainly the toughest that Sandy had ever experienced. The going was very rough, the bush very thick and now mopani flies added to the misery of the tsetse bites. Water was in very short supply and had to be strictly rationed. Food was not exactly gourmet and sleeping at nights uncomfortable to put it mildly and fairly dangerous so that one of them had to be awake at all times. Matters were not improved either by mosquitoes taking over from their daytime friends, the tsetse and mopani flies, to make sleep increasingly difficult.

Only once in all of those three days did they catch a glimpse of the bull and he spotted them long before they saw him and went crashing off with his usual snort of disgust. With water and food now finished they spent the fourth day finding their way back to camp. As Sandy sank into his chair he said quite quietly, "I think we'll all have a break tomorrow and stay here – OK, Tony?"

"I thought you'd never suggest it!" replied a very relieved Tony and then added also quite quietly, "Sandy, there are other bulls, you know. This is a very good area for buffalo and Wambua tells me there are some big herds a mile or two downstream so I am sure we can pick up a decent head there and forget about your old 'Dagga Boy'."

Sandy had been sitting with his eyes closed as the whisky started doing its stuff but at Tony's remark his eyes shot open.

"No, no way. I want that old bull – nothing else will do. I'll be OK after a day's rest."

He did feel better after remaining in camp all day, while Tony went out and shot an impala, more to feed the staff than themselves. Then they took the Land Rover back to the area where they had last seen the bull and scoured the whole place for any sign of him. At one of the very few remaining water-holes they did find his spoor. They were now far from the river and the old boy had to water somewhere.

"What about lying in ambush here for a day?" suggested Sandy. It was not a bad idea in itself but Sandy wanted Tony to agree because even after this one day of rest he was feeling very weak. Those cancer cells were at work deep in his body, of that he was sure.

"OK, not a bad idea, worth a try anyway," Sandy was relieved to hear.

They constructed a hide some 50 yards from the waterhole in as thick a piece of bush as they could find where the wind blew [hopefully !] from the waterhole towards them, then early the next morning did a big detour and crept into the hide and lay still.

It is not easy to remain totally still *and* alert for any length of time just sitting in an armchair. To do so in the heat of the Zambezi valley while lying on your stomach on a rough, stony surface with tsetses and mopani flies biting you is impossible. Soon after midday the bull did come to the waterhole. He approached from the right at an angle that was difficult for those in the hide to see. Wambua sensed the presence of the animal before he could see it and tried to convey this to Sandy. At that moment Sandy was actually holding his breath to try and stifle any noise as a spasm of pain shot through his lower abdomen. He let out his breath as silently as possible and tried to look in the direction that Wambua was indicating.

He did see a dark form moving slowly some two hundred yards to his right but definitely approaching the waterhole so he shifted slightly to be able to use his rifle should the possibility arise. As he moved a grey lourie, or 'go away bird' as they are known due to their raucous call of *'goway, goway',* rose from a nearby tree. The distant dark form immediately stopped then, as the ruddy bird screamed again, turned and bolted away. The hunted animal's best friend had warned the quarry again just in time.

"What now?" It was a good question put by all three of them simultaneously. But one thing was becoming more and more apparent – Sandy's desire to get this wily old bull was increasing rather than the other way round. After another day's rest the three of them were on the trail of the bull for each of the next seven days. In all that time they only saw him twice more and never got a chance of a shot.

Then it was the last day and, after another abortive day in the hills, Sandy, Tony and Wambua were back in camp by four o' clock and, apart from the two shots at the francolin, Sandy had not fired a shot for all of the three weeks.

While Tony chose to remain in camp and organise things for an early departure from the valley in the morning, Sandy said he would like just to wander along the riverbank quietly on his own. He wanted to listen to the river, watch the hippos wallowing in the shallows, spot the odd croc and maybe hear the fish eagle calling far away across the water. Out of habit he took his rifle with him. It could – probably would – be the last time he would be able to do this. The last days had been a real struggle. He had gritted his teeth and not complained but suspected that Tony knew he had a real problem.

Disappointment was certainly there at his failure to get the bull but what a paradise the Zambezi valley was – still very much as God had made it. His reverie was suddenly interrupted by a movement on the edge of some reeds quite near where he had originally shot the two francolins so long ago. He stopped.

Out of the reeds emerged the biggest bull buffalo Sandy had ever seen. It was 'his 'bull – there was no question about that. The wind blew gently in his face, the sun shone low in the sky from behind him and the old bull had no idea he was there. It stopped, raised its massive head with the spectacular horns curving majestically down on each side.

Sandy, feeling remarkably calm, raised his trusty double-barrelled Winchester .458 and took a bead just behind the bull's shoulder. He couldn't miss – not from fifty yards. The bull raised his head a little bit more and the great liquid eyes seemed to look straight at Sandy.

Sandy took up the first pressure on the trigger – then, very slowly he lowered the rifle, took off his hat and threw it at the bull shouting, "Thanks for a super three weeks, you old bastard!" With the traditional snort the old bull whirled round and galloped away.

"Nice walk?" asked Tony.

"Lovely," replied Sandy, "saw a fish eagle."

Sandy died of cancer of the colon a short six months later. He had never fired another shot and now his disarmed .458 hangs in the blank space on the library wall where a magnificent buffalo's head might have hung.

22
The Raffle

We do not often go to the races and even more seldom have a bet if we ever do. However, we were all encouraged to go last week as the meeting had been sponsored by a wealthy parent at the school attended by our children and was to be used to raise funds for the school's dilapidated playing fields.

My children enjoy their sport so we were more than pleased to attend the meeting and contribute our share to what we considered a worthy cause.

It was a lovely day and a good crowd soon in evidence. Our school had a special marquee in the centre of the course and lunch was being served at long buffet tables as we arrived. We paid for this and sat down at a table with other parents who we knew slightly. It seemed that they knew a lot more about racing than we did and eagerly perused the race card and offered advice on which horses they thought would win.

"Fork Lightening in the 3-30 is an absolute cinch and what about Calypso Magic in the main race – that's owned by Jimmy Crouch's parents, you know, the boy with red hair in our children's class."

There was a tote nearby and a couple of bookies had set up their stalls near our marquee so it would have been very easy to place a bet on either of these horses as recommended by our friends. However, we felt that by doing this we would be supporting the racecourse [or bookie!] and not the school so, despite the exhortations of our table companions, we resisted this temptation and instead bought a ticket in a raffle, all proceeds of which would go to the school. The raffle was for a large hamper of food and drink containing all manner of desirable goodies like malt whisky, Belgian chocolates and vintage wine. The pretty girl selling the tickets assured us that the draw would take place in the marquee where we were sitting immediately after the last race.

As I was about to put the ticket in the little diary that I keep in my hip pocket together with driving licence, credit cards etc., I glanced down at it and happened to catch sight of the number. I don't know about you, but I never usually look at the number of a raffle ticket until the winning number is about to be announced and only then do I check what it is. However, on this occasion the number was instantly recognisable as it happened to be the date of my birthday and, what is more, had my initial in front of the number. It was: M9970. Thinking no more about it I stowed it away in the diary from whence I felt sure it would finally end up in the waste-paper basket at home. I can't remember ever having won a raffle.

Lunch being finished we felt we had better actually see something of the racing so wandered down to the paddock in time to watch the horses parade for the main race of the day. We soon picked out number 5, Calypso Magic, and there, standing in the middle of the paddock was a small boy with red hair obviously 'attached' to a very smart couple in earnest conversation with a very small man [not much larger than the small boy, in fact], wearing a brightly coloured orange and brown silk shirt, white britches and small shiny, black boots.

"That's the jockey," said my wife. Really!

Another worried looking man hovered on the periphery of this little group interrupting the conversation from time to time with hurried comments and much shaking of the right index finger. "That's the trainer," I thought, mentally trumping my wife's knowledge. Circling this lot were a number of magnificent looking horses all with gleaming coats and very much on their toes [do horses have toes?] while the grooms leading them tried to keep them under control.

Despite ourselves, we were fascinated by this little tableau and had not really noticed that quite a crowd had gathered behind us and, as we turned to go, there was quite a lot of jostling and I was pushed slightly in the back. Nothing serious and we climbed the grandstand to watch the race.

Obviously we followed the fortunes of number 5 , Calypso Magic, but despite vigorous waving of the short whip and screams from most of the people around us, the little man in orange and brown was unable to persuade his mount to go fast enough to overtake an equally small man in pink and black riding a lovely looking grey horse. So, much to the disappointment of our fellow watchers and the financial detriment of our lunchtime companions, Calypso Magic finished only second. We smiled at each other and mentally congratulated ourselves on not having followed the well-meaning advice that had been offered.

We did watch another couple of races before drifting back to the marquee for a drink prior to going home and, we suddenly remembered, to hear the result of the raffle.

Light lager in hand, we suddenly heard a loud banging on a table and a well-dressed man in a bowler hat held his hand up for silence. He was approached by the same pretty girl who had sold us the raffle ticket and she was now carrying a large earthenware pot which the bowler-hatted man informed us contained all the counterfoils of the raffle tickets sold to us that day and, "thank you very much for contributing to this worthy cause." He then asked us all to check our tickets as this 'wonderful prize' would only be handed over on presentation of the ticket matching the number drawn from the earthenware pot.

Hastily I reached into my hip pocket to retrieve the ticket [although I still well remembered the number]. Horror of horrors, the pocket was empty! I tried every other pocket just in case I had put the little diary into a different one by mistake. Nothing. It couldn't have fallen out – it never had and anyway I always fastened the flap down with the Velcro strip provided for this very purpose. So where on earth was it? Then it dawned on me. I had been robbed. Pickpocketed to be exact. And I clearly remembered where and when this must have happened – as we tried to leave the paddock just before the main race. In all that jostling someone had flipped up the Velcro, put their fingers into the hip pocket and easily removed the diary. My wife had always told me that pocket was a stupid place to keep anything remotely valuable.

I really could not have cared less about the raffle ticket but my driving licence and all my credit cards had now also been stolen – what a pain. Meanwhile silence had fallen on the assembled multitude and the pretty girl was holding up the earthenware pot like some sort of sacred offering and 'Bowler Hat', with a great show of pulling up his sleeve and shutting his eyes, was putting his hand into the pot to withdraw the winning ticket.

"And the winning number is M9970. Would the lucky holder of that ticket please bring it up here and I will hand over this magnificent prize?"

A dapper little middle-aged man, who I had never seen before, rose smiling from a nearby table. Waving the ticket in the air and acknowledging some disappointed applause, he made his way up to 'Bowler Hat'.

Somewhat to my own surprise I suddenly found myself shouting, "Hey! That's my ticket."

People nearby stopped clapping and looked disapprovingly at me. Don't be stupid – you could almost hear them saying – if it were your ticket you would be taking it up to claim the prize and not that gentleman.

But I was convinced – that smarmy little bastard had picked my pocket and, not only was he claiming my prize, but he had all my cards and addresses as well. I hate making a fuss and am embarrassed about making a spectacle of myself but I was angry and had already started something. More people were staring at me and I found myself on my feet. My wife was hissing, "Sit down". The room fell silent and 'Bowler Hat' paused in the act of shaking the hand of 'the winner'.

"What's all this about?" he said, "This certainly appears to be the ticket number M9970 which corresponds with the number which I withdrew from the pot."

"But I bought that ticket," I shouted and started walking towards him. "Didn't I?" I added, appealing to the pretty girl. She, of course, had sold lots of tickets and could not possibly remember everyone who had purchased one and certainly not which particular one. She just shrugged – quite prettily – but it didn't help.

'Bowler Hat' looked down his nose at me and, indicating 'Smarmy Bastard', said, "Are you accusing this man of stealing your ticket?"

This was a bit of a poser and brought me to my senses smartish. If I said 'yes' I would be making a very serious accusation and I had no way of proving it. But I could hardly meekly back down now. My thoughts were interrupted by 'Bowler Hat' saying, "I presume you have reported this to the police, so perhaps we should call them in."

I hadn't, of course, as I had only discovered the loss this minute. Then I had a brainwave.

"Can I ask this gentleman," I said, indicating 'Smarmy Bastard', "to empty his pockets to see if he also has my diary, credit cards and driving licence which were in it together with the raffle ticket?"

I said that I hated making a spectacle of myself but now I was going overboard. There was murmuring all round the marquee and people were leaving their seats and edging closer. 'Bowler Hat' looked confused and angry. He had not bargained for this sort of thing when agreeing to conduct the raffle draw. I glanced at 'Smarmy Bastard' and was shaken to find him quietly smiling.

"Sure," he said, "have a look." And he meticulously started turning his pockets inside out. Some loose change, a handkerchief, a couple of losing betting slips, a small note book and the stub of a pencil soon formed a heap on the table but not a sign of my diary or any of its contents.

He stood there with his arms outstretched, all his pockets with the linings showing and a supercilious grin on his face. I could think of nothing to say.

One can sense a shift of emotion in any audience and there was certainly one now. From being mildly curious this audience was rapidly becoming actively hostile and I could hear mutterings such as – 'For God's sake shut up', 'It's only a bloody raffle' and 'What the hell is he getting at?' Added to this my wife's hissing had also taken on a more sinister note and she was actually tugging at my shirt sleeve.

I slunk from the marquee, strode to our car and drove home in icy silence.

A few days later a small parcel arrived in the post. On opening it I found it to contain one bar of Belgian chocolate. There was no address given by the sender.

23
What Result?

The final of our local Golf Club Championships was contested between two men who did not really like each other very much. Or rather, not to put too fine a point on it, two people who loathed each other's guts!

Hamish Lumsden was a dour Scot, getting on a bit now but a long-standing and respected member of the club – indeed, a one-time captain. A bit old fashioned but a stickler for tradition and a very keen competitor. Luke Brooksbank was still quite young, a new member of the club, very rich, ambitious and more than a little pleased with himself. His hedge fund company was prospering nicely and membership to this fine old club was definitely a step in the right social direction.

The two men had absolutely nothing in common except that they were both very good at golf. This fact alone could have at least made them accept each other for what they were had not Luke, playing immediately behind Hamish one day, sent his drive sailing past that four ball and very narrowly missing old Hamish himself. Hamish stood his ground and waited for Luke to come up to him, expecting a fulsome apology which he was debating whether to accept or not.

Luke, on getting within fifty metres merely shouted, "Sorry about that, old boy, but I do wish you old codgers would get a move on."

'Old boy!' 'Old codgers', Hamish was speechless with indignation. Failing to come up with any suitable reply, he just stalked off saying nothing but bristling with rage, which was not improved by his overhearing Luke mutter to his banking partner, "Silly old fart!"

Hamish reported the matter to his friends on the committee, but got little satisfaction when they said there was really nothing they could do. Driving into the four ball in front was very bad manners but did, unfortunately, happen quite often and the offender in this case had actually said 'sorry'.

Shortly after this Luke wanted to present a trophy to the club entitled, 'The Luke Brooksbank Perpetual Challenge Trophy' for a Stableford Alliance competition. Hamish thought this an incredibly ostentatious name for a somewhat obscure competition and used his influence with his friends on the committee to persuade them to reject Luke's offer. This infuriated Luke because he had already spent quite a lot of money buying the large, ornate trophy in anticipation of it being accepted with fawning gratitude. He knew full well who had influenced the committee's decision.

It was, therefore, a very tense little party that teed off at the start of the final of the club's match play tournament. Both men had employed a caddy for the occasion, foregoing their normal practice of pulling their own cart. "Two pairs of eyes are better than one to keep an eye on that bounder," Hamish had observed to his friends when explaining why he was indulging in such an unusual extravagance. "I could well need a little helpful advice to beat that crafty old sod," confided Luke to his banking mates.

Luke with all the new equipment, plus youth and strength on his side consistently out drove old Hamish by some distance but Hamish, using his faithful old clubs [just one step removed from the original hickory shafted design!], was more often on the fairway as Luke's extravagant drives sometimes soared into the rough.

In icy silence they proceeded through 17 holes each briefly taking the lead only to have to surrender it after an all too brief tenure. So as they stood on the 18th and final tee box they were all square. The 18th hole was a comparatively straightforward par 4, not too long and dead straight. But just past the 200 metre marker was a clump of trees close to the left hand side of the fairway. They were tall pine trees with quite a dense covering of undergrowth at ground level but a few clearings in the copse did sometimes provide a view of the green some 160 metres away. Nevertheless it was not the ideal place to go.

Hamish, having the honour, drove first. A conservative 190 metres straight down the middle leaving himself about 160 metres to the flag which was the perfect distance for his trusty 5 wood. Luke, unsheathing his Callaway Big Bertha, launched into his drive hoping for just a wedge to the flag. But, horror of horrors, he hooked the drive and it careered off into the pine trees on the left.

In silence Hamish took a quick look at the lie of his own ball, did not play his shot but went first to help find his opponent's ball. This, of course, was only common courtesy on any golf course no matter who your opponent was. Obviously Luke's ball had hit a tree and could be anywhere, so the two players and the two caddies split up with a view to covering the whole area while trying to find the ball within the five minutes permitted in the rules.

Hamish took a quick look at his watch – five minutes was the rule and five minutes it would be as far as he was concerned. There being no referee to monitor the time, he broke his silence and called out to Luke, "Five minutes from now – I make it exactly five minutes to three." He received a muffled, "OK."

The pine trees were scattered into small groups extending over a considerable area so for a lot of the time the four searchers were out of sight of each other. Hamish glanced down at his watch – thirty seconds to go. Then, out of the corner of his eye, he spotted a ball. The make of the ball was facing up – Titleist 2, the very same as the one he knew Luke to be using. It must be his ball. Then he saw the two small blue dots that Luke had shown him as his own special mark. Hamish looked at his watch again – fifteen seconds to go. With a quick glance round to confirm that no one was looking, he bent down, picked up the ball and put it in his pocket.

Ten seconds to go and he hurried off looking for Luke. He saw him some 15 metres away with his back turned and was about to announce that the time was up and a lost ball must be declared, when Luke whirled round and shouted, "Found it!"

Stunned, Hamish walked over to where Luke was standing with a satisfied grin on his face and, looking down, saw a very clean Titleist 2 with two blue marks prominently displayed. The ball was lying in a small glade with a clear view to the green a mere 140 metres away.

Hamish thought, 'The young bastard has put another ball down but I can't say anything because his original ball is in my pocket'.

Luke thought, 'Got away with it! The silly old sod was about to call time up and declare the ball lost.'

SO WHAT HAPPENED NEXT?

1st possibility:

Hamish, without a word, turned his back on Luke and headed back towards his own ball on the fairway. Halfway there and still in the pine trees he casually dropped the ball in his pocket into a patch of rough grass behind a tree. He stopped and called back to Luke. "Just come over here a moment. Are you sure you have got the right ball? This looks like the one you were playing with."

Luke hesitated, and then wandered slowly over. Clearly disconcerted, he looked with horror at the ball nestling in the clump of grass. "As this ball is now dead, why not pick it up and identify it," said Hamish grimly. Unwillingly, Luke did just that and when both caddies confirmed that it was indeed the ball that Luke had played off the tee, there was no denying it.

The match was immediately forfeited and Hamish was declared Club Champion.

Luke was asked to resign from the club for cheating. Hamish 'forgot' to have his name engraved on the trophy and shortly after gave up golf.

2nd possibility:

Hamish, without a word, turned his back on Luke and headed back towards his own ball on the fairway. When he reached it he took out his trusty 5 wood and went for the green. But he was upset and preoccupied so sliced the approach shot badly into some long grass on the right of the green. Luke then had his shot. The lie was good and he could see the flag. His 7 iron shot flew high and true landing a mere 2 metres from the hole. Hamish hacked out of the long grass to the edge of the green and two putted from there to be down in five. Luke calmly rolled in his putt for a birdie and victory.

Luke took no time at all in having his name engraved on the trophy but was angry to discover, a few days after putting it back in its place of honour in the clubhouse, that a nasty scratch had somehow appeared right across his name.

3rd possibility:

Hamish, without a word, turned his back on Luke and headed back towards his own ball on the fairway. When he reached it he took out his trusty 5 wood and hit the ball squarely onto the middle of the green. Luke then had his shot. Although the lie was good and he could see the flag, he again hooked his shot and the ball bounced into the left hand bunker. Advantage, Hamish. Luke played a reasonable bunker shot but his ball was still just beyond Hamish's ball and on the same line to the hole – but he had played 3 shots to Hamish's two and was still further away. "Mark your ball, would you?" he said. No 'please' or anything like that. Hamish, reaching into his pocket for the marker, forgot that there was a golf ball in there and, in withdrawing the marker, accidentally brought out the ball as well. It fell onto the green, bounced twice and came to rest not a metre from where Luke was waiting to putt. Facing upwards and clearly visible in the afternoon sun were the words 'Titleist 2', and close to that two blue dots.

Both players stared at the ball aghast. Both players knew exactly what the other had done. Without a word they both picked up their balls and stalked off the green. The Club Championship that year was declared void.

26
A Tame Honey Badger

Stories abound about weird and wonderful wild animals kept as pets, particularly in Africa. I have known of monkeys, baboons, various antelope, cheetahs, warthogs, hyenas, otters and even hippos, elephants, rhinos and snakes. I spent most of my life in Kenya and Zimbabwe and had a fair selection of those myself but there was one very special one which very few people would consider a suitable pet.

Undoubtedly the most interesting wild animal that I ever had as a pet was a honey badger [mellivora capensis]. Not everybody's choice by a long shot! The honey badger or ratel which is an Afrikaans word derived from the Dutch for a rattle after the curious noise it makes, is generally regarded as the most fearless and ferocious animal in Africa and, pound for pound, the most dangerous. It is a squat, strong little animal weighing between 20 and 35 pounds in the males and 11to 22 pounds for females, but the main feature is an incredibly thick, very loose skin. When ours was a year old I could pick it up by the scruff of the neck and it could still turn round inside its skin and bite me. No dog or cat can do that. It is this thick skin that makes it virtually impervious to bee stings and therefore able to raid bee's nests for the honey that it loves so much and provides part of its name.

Stories abound about this little animal attacking foes as large as a buffalo if they thought their young were threatened. Knowing they were no match in size, they have the nasty habit of going straight for the testicles of any larger male animal – a very effective ploy. Robert Ruark, that well-known American author of novels based in Kenya [*Something of Value* and *Uhuru*] entitled his autobiography, *The Honey Badger*, his reasoning being that, as it was mainly about the women in his life, it was a reasonable title. I wonder why?

We were farming in Zimbabwe when our cattle herder came in one day with a very small, rat like little thing in the palm of his hand. It was dark grey all over and its eyes were tightly closed. It was obviously very young and could only crawl a little bit like a very small puppy. We had no idea what it was.

We took it in and fed it cow's milk through a dropper and a nutritious type of baby food. It was always hungry and responded very readily to any affection or food and never looked like dying or even becoming ill from this obviously strange diet. It slept in a small dog basket inside a cage. This was to protect it more from our own dogs rather than to restrain it. During the day, while we were around, it first crawled and then ran round the house tending to try and follow one or other of us.

After about two months it started to change colour, becoming a lighter grey on top and darker underneath and it was only then that we suddenly realised we had a baby honey badger on our hands. Later the colours changed even more to be the traditional white on top and black underneath. I was recently married at the time and had two small boys; Robert aged three and Harry, 18 months. Their favourite book at the time was about Ferdinand the bull in Spain being taken to fight in the bullring in Madrid. So, rather inappropriately, we christened our honey badger Madrid, which soon became Madriddy!

It soon became apparent that Madriddy was a male and he continued to thrive. We continued to feed him a fairly special diet but we soon realised that he would eat almost anything. He grew strong quite quickly and was soon ragging with our dogs and more than holding his own, so he no longer slept in his cage but just had a basket like them. He was extremely affectionate and hated not being with us. Indeed, if we tried to shut him out of the room he went to incredible lengths to get back in, scratching at the door and even prising open a badly fitting door by hooking his claws under the bottom and pulling. We once locked him behind an eight foot wall but he immediately climbed up it and just dropped down the other side landing on his back – I have pictures of him doing just this.

He came for walks with us every evening when we took the dogs and was never on a lead or restrained in any way. Once he was ragging with our Pekinese and became a little too rough so my wife flicked him with the jersey she was carrying and shouted at him to behave. He was mortified and came rushing up to her, jumped into her arms and sucked his back foot while making little grunty noises as if to say 'sorry'.

He became particularly attached to my younger son, Harry, who used to cuddle him and play endlessly. This became a bit of a problem because he soon insisted on sleeping in Harry's bed and, short of locking him up in a cage, we could not stop this. He objected very strongly to being put in any sort of cage, made a filthy noise all the time and chewed at the door, often managing to open it. He was incredibly strong.

He hated to be left alone so much that we used to take him in the car with us and when going to play squash at the club he would come along and watch, amusing the spectators waiting for a game by climbing all over them. Up to the age of one year he never showed any sign of aggression at all and was always most friendly. But as he got older he did occasionally start to lose his temper when getting the worst of a rag with the dogs. He never actually bit them in anger, but, knowing their reputation, it was a little worrying. I was worried about him sleeping in Harry's bed, fearing that Harry might roll over or kick him in his sleep, so provoking a bite to the area they were most reputed to go for!

There was no way we could have returned him to the wild, he just would not go, so we contacted an animal rescue centre which took in hurt or sick wild animals. It was a charity centre called Chipangali Orphanage owned by someone called Viv Wilson and situated near Bulawayo. We rang Viv up and asked if he could take our honey badger. He knew of no one who had ever owned such an unlikely pet and was glad to take him.

On our advice Viv never locked him up and he just ran round his sort of zoo completely free. Viv did a weekly television programme at that time to try and raise funds and soon Madriddy became a star of that show. Viv could not handle his odd name so renamed him 'Cheeky' and as such he became known to thousands of TV viewers throughout the country. He remained with Viv for five years until one day he was just not there. A week later he re-appeared looking rather pleased with himself. He had found a mate in the wild.

From then on he lived a sort of dual existence. He never introduced his wife to Viv but just came and went as he pleased. His visits became less and less frequent until finally they ceased altogether. No one really ever found out what happened to him but I trust and hope he was happy. He was a truly amazing pet to have had and whatever their reputation, I retain a very soft spot for honey badgers.

For all that, you still can't beat a dog. Whoever started having them as a pet certainly got it right!

25

A Day at the Olympics

On a day in early August 1948 I went to Wembley Stadium, London, to watch a day of athletics in the Olympic Games. On Tuesday 7th August 2012 [64 years later] I went to the brand new Olympic Stadium in Stratford, London, to watch an evening of athletics in the Olympic Games. In 1948 it was just after the war and it was known as 'the Austerity Games'. Athletes stayed in private houses or hotels and went to the stadium on a London bus with a packet of sandwiches for their lunch. When it got dark, and the discus finals were unfinished, spectators were asked to bring their cars in and turn the headlights on so as to see where the discuses were landing! A ticket cost six shillings and six pence for a full day of athletics. I was one of a few thousand actually to see the competition [virtually no TV in those days].

What a difference 64 years makes. In 2012 I was one of 80,000 in the stadium plus a couple of billion watching on TV. It is already being hailed as the greatest Olympics ever and I can well believe it will be. Tickets for the two and a half hour evening athletics session cost £95.

Some winning time comparisons –

	1948	2012
100 metres	10.30	9.63
10,000 metres	29.59	27.01
High Jump	1.98 [6'5']	2.38 [7'8']

I watched those three events in 1948 and Emil Zatopek, who won the 10,000 metres and lapped all but two of his opponents, was hailed as one of the greatest long-distance runners ever. If anyone ran at his speed today they would be lapped!

What will times be in another 64 years?

One could go on making comparisons for ever but you get the picture – they were poles apart. Actually, to see exactly what was going on in the athletics arena it was much easier on TV. The coverage was excellent with very knowledgeable commentators. Sitting in the stands one could not even see the number on an athlete's back. There was a big screen at each end and a continual commentary over the public address system but the actual athletes were remote 'pin men'. But that is not the point. The word 'atmosphere' is the one most used and this cannot be canned – it was magic!

I was given a ticket by Charles Shaw and went up to London by bus. I was met at the terminal by Charles' daughter, Alex – bus to her flat in Fulham where we had a quick lunch with her boyfriend, Andy. Then we went by underground to Waterloo where we met Charles. Together with the Olympic ticket we all had an underground ticket valid to go anywhere on that day. From Waterloo to Stratford the coaches were pretty crowded – full of happy, smiling people, many draped in a variety of flags most of which were Union Jacks. There was one huge figure near us and when he turned round he was revealed to be a member of the US rowing team.

Disembarking at Stratford we were greeted by a pristine station bedecked with flags and posters and purple-clad volunteers offering any assistance needed. There was regularly one perched on a stepladder with a loud-hailer directing the flow of humanity in the right direction. Occasionally some sort of Man Mountain would amble by and there would be a burst of music and the person on the stepladder would yell, 'Welcome to Team Kazakhstan's weight lifter.' Everyone would shout and clap, upon which the Man Mountain would raise his arms and acknowledge the applause with a big grin.

Nearing the actual stadium the solid stream of people split into several smaller ones and we were ushered into security check areas exactly like those when one boards a flight. These were conducted by the army. I had forgotten to leave my Swiss penknife behind and this was swiftly removed from me. I looked sad and asked how I could get it back [I've had it a very long time]. The offending article was passed to the sergeant-in-charge who looked me up and down, winked, handed back the knife and said," You don't look the type to cut anyone's throat, but keep that ruddy thing well hidden." Nice gesture.

We were early for the evening's events so had over an hour to wander round the whole complex which contained not only the main stadium, but a host of others as well – velodrome, swimming pools, basket ball, warm-up areas, food areas and the whole Olympic village to name a few. Huge wide paved streets bisected the whole place and even with well over 150,000 people wandering around, one was never crowded. More flags and fancy dress from a multitude of different countries, little side shows of children running races and the winner being hoisted onto a soap box and having a 'medal' put round their neck while we all sang the National Anthem amid roars of laughter and applause.

We had brought a picnic supper and sat eating this at one of the extensive food areas. Again, no scrum, plenty of tables and seats available with food and drink, including alcohol, readily available if you had not brought your own. Some half an hour before the events were due to start we bought a programme and entered the stadium to look for our seats. Emerging from the top of the stairs at the level of these seats we were suddenly greeted by our first view of the interior of this magnificent stadium. Stunning! You will all have seen pictures of this on the TV but this totally fails to do justice to the spectacle as we emerged from the darkness of the stairway into the brilliantly lit stadium with the huge flame burning at one end.

I will not go into the actual results of all we saw, these have all been well documented – suffice it to say that whenever a British athlete [Team GB] entered the stadium, was introduced before a race, passed successive sections of the crowd or did anything special, the crescendo of cheering could not fail to inspire the most insensitive of beings, no wonder the team reaped an unprecedented haul of medals. Final event that day was the 1,500 metres, an event at which Charles had once aspired to run for South Africa having run the mile in a fraction over 4 minutes back in the '70s. In between events there were medal ceremonies and we all duly stood to attention and remained silent while some weird National Anthems were played.

As the final event ended 80,000 people rose as one and headed for a variety of exits but all aimed at one of only three gates out of the fenced off Olympic area. My heart sank and I looked at my watch – 9.20pm.

When on earth would we get back to the flat competing with this mob and it wasn't only the 80,000 from the main stadium – there were plenty of other people around outside. Midnight, if we were lucky.

We were home by ten-thirty! We streamed back to the underground where all the entrances were open, no ticket required, and a succession of trains just kept coming. We crammed on to one and joined the happy, jostling crowd. Made a couple of changes and the mob thinned. As we boarded our 3rd train a young man who was already seated, leaped up and offered me his seat – I didn't realise I looked THAT old! But what a nice gesture and typical of the attitude of everybody. As we neared our destination the train suddenly braked violently and threw a young lady plonk onto my lap. Everyone roared with laughter – I immediately stood up and said, "If you want my seat that badly, please have it!" More roars of laughter from the whole carriage. Out we got at the next station, caught a taxi straight away and back at the flat in just over an hour – fantastic.

Great day. Wish Nikki had been with me but she met me off the bus in Wincanton next day having been out to lunch the day before with friends who completely understood why I had rudely excused myself from their party. You don't miss an opportunity like that and I was not about to. But a huge thank you to Charles and Sonia who had got the tickets.

24
The Ultimate Embarrassment

I am not very good on a computer and fear I never will be but did get to the stage when I rather fancied myself. E-mails are a wonderful, quick way of communicating and, as my hand-writing is somewhat worse than my computer skills, I do use them a lot. I even learned how to send 'attachments' and this was a wonderful thing too. I could type something out, make quite sure I had got it absolutely right, save it and be able to send a pre-typed, correct e-mail immediately. Great as long as I wanted to say the same thing to everyone whenever I sent an e-mail. So no good to replace a chatty letter but if I wanted to send a circular, for example, to several people it was ideal.

So, when my cousin in Yorkshire asked me to try and sell his oven-ready grouse for him in the South of England I said that I would and typed out a list of people who I knew and who might be tempted into buying this delicacy. This I headed 'GROUSE', pressed 'save' and put safely in my 'documents' folder. I felt rather pleased with myself as I now had the list easily accessible and would be able to refer to it and add to it as new people came to mind.

I then typed out a letter to send to the people on my list and 'saved' that. But I needed more than this to persuade them to buy some grouse, so I scanned an article that my cousin had had printed extolling the wonders of his grouse, headed it 'GROUSE ARTICLE' and managed to save this as well. I was doing really well now and nearly ready to start sending a batch of e-mails out to my selected customers.

But first I thought I had better go through my list of possible customers and decide who would be most likely to buy. I brought up my 'GROUSE' file and beside each name I added a comment concerning their likelihood of buying. Then I was ready to go.

I brought up the e-mail address of each name in turn, wrote a short, personal introductory few lines and attached the scanned copy of my cousin's article, pressed 'send' and off they went. Feeling very pleased with myself by now I awaited replies to come flooding in with a mountain of orders. A very few did and these all contained a pretty brief sort of 'No thanks'.

This rather concerned me. Had I said enough about how difficult it was to buy such quality? Did I need to explain a bit more about what a grouse tasted like? Had I targeted the right selection of people? All sorts of doubts started worrying me as it seemed that my cousin was getting plenty of orders coming in. I went to my 'sent' column and brought up a sample e-mail that I had sent to a couple who I knew slightly from a nearby village called Ed and Moira Figginshaw. I read through the few lines that I had written introducing the product – these seemed quite clear and good so what could the problem be? I clicked on to the copy of my cousin's article that I had attached just to refresh my memory as to what he had said.

Up came the attachment headed 'GROUSE' and there followed, not the article, but a long list of names with comments beside each one. I had pressed the wrong attachment! I should have pressed 'GROUSE ARTICLE'. Wow! I scrolled down to Figginshaw to see what I had written beside their name and the blood flooded to my face as I read – 'Figginshaw, Ed and Moira, grumpy old sod but greedy and plenty of cash, should buy.' In horror I looked further down my list to Murray, Nigel and Ann, mean as hell, not much chance. Then Thurston, Mike, lonely old bachelor [not surprised!] but might buy. I hardly dared look any further but did and read that I regarded Tim and Angela as boring stick-in-the-muds but would possibly like to serve grouse at a dinner party to create an impression. Tim and Angela Stephenson were my *next door neighbours!* And Geoff Wilson, who I played golf with, was deemed to be a likely buyer but very suspect payer.

What would you do? I need help.

1] Write to each person in turn and apologise

2] Laugh it off as a joke
3] Commit suicide
4] Blame it all on somebody else
5] Send everyone a brace of free grouse

Actually this story has not been written from my erstwhile home. I am now in Canada and unlikely to return.